THE
TWENTY-TWO
GATES
TO
THE GARDEN

THE
TWENTY-TWO
GATES
TO
THE GARDEN

Steven M. Rosman

Illustrated by Josepha Silman

JASON ARONSON INC.
Northvale, New Jersey
London

This book was set in 16 pt. Berkeley Old Style by Alpha Graphics of Pittsfield, New Hampshire, and printed by Haddon Craftsmen in Scranton, Pennsylvania.

Library of Congress Cataloging-in-Publication Data
Rosman, Steven M.
    The twenty-two gates to the garden / by Steven M. Rosman.
        p.   cm.
    Summary: Original tales inspired by kabbalistic tradition.
    ISBN 1-56821-124-4
    1. Children's stories, American.   2. Cabala—Juvenile fiction.
    [1. Cabala—Fiction.   2. Short stories.]   I. Title.   II. Title: 22
    gates to the garden.
    PZ7.R71954Tw   1994
    [Fic]—dc20   93-35944 √

Manufactured in the United States of America. Jason Aronson Inc. offers books and cassettes. For information and catalog write to Jason Aronson Inc., 230 Livingston Street, Northvale, New Jersey 07647.

I dedicate this book to the most blessed miracles in my life: the love and devotion of my wife, Bari, and children, Michal (Mikki) and Ilan. They have taught me more about wonder and the presence of the sacred than the greatest of my great teachers. Most often, I hear God's voice in their loving tones and I feel God's nearness in the embrace of their affection. They are God's answers to the prayers I am sure I offered before I was a soul incarnated. So to Bari, Mikki, and Ilan, I say thank you and then, in more hushed and reverent tones, I whisper Amen.

Contents

Contents

Preface

This book is a collection of tales drawn from my studies and experience of kabbalistic tradition and from the wisdom of my many teachers. Each tale is a gateway to a world of mystery and discovery, and each offers the reader a chance to see his or her world anew.

Inside these covers and upon these pages live age-old teachings of kabbalistic tradition that are given voice by the tales' main characters: a king and a queen, a prince and a princess, and a remarkable teacher. Oh, there is a gardener and an old man, too. And, where else would such encounters with such marvel and mystery occur if not in a garden, my analogue to the *Pardes* or "Mystical Orchard" of classical kabbalistic lore. There a princess is challenged to see her world as if for the first time. There she learns to see the light in every darkness. There a prince discovers that some of life's wonders cannot be explained; rather they might only be experienced firsthand. There two children come to realize that they are part of a universe and the universe is part of them. There death is the means by which life is expanded. There wisdom is revealed and pretension exposed. There young children come to see that appearance can be illusory and truth often concealed.

While inspired by the wisdom of the Jewish mystical tradition, these tales have been written to grant anyone who wishes entrance to its enriching and profound spiritual teachings. The gates are open to all who want to enter: no matter his background; no matter her prior studies; no matter their particular religious heritage.

While written with the hope that one generation will share these tales with another, the text might be enjoyed by older or younger readers individually. And while written by a storyteller for storytelling, the tales might be shared among participants in study circles or by teachers with their students.

And so: "In the beginning there was a Garden and a Palace. Twenty-two gates opened to the Garden. . . ."

Welcome.

*   *   *

Note: Additional information about several of the stories can be found in the Notes section at the end of book.

Acknowledgments

I hope that this book will open doorways to the mysterious and wondrous that surround us every moment of every day. Perhaps the most significant miracle of all is that this book was born through the imaginative and visionary genius of my publisher and mentor, Arthur Kurzweil. What you see in the pages that follow does not conform to my original proposal. Thanks to Arthur's confidence in me and his marvelous ability to bring forth from his authors wonders about which they were not previously aware, this collection of stories was conceived and eventually nursed to birth. I am grateful to Arthur's constant support and unfailing encouragement. For that I am blessed.

Acknowledgments

I am blessed, as well, for the presence in my life of extraordinary people who have graced these stories with generous gifts of their talents and the mastery of their crafts:

Josepha Silman has adorned these pages with her remarkable artistry. It is a most difficult task, indeed, to endeavor to render the spiritual in the form of matter. Yet Josepha did so with exquisite art that evokes a sense of the ineffable and connects us to the teachers, past and present, who guide us on our sacred paths.

Muriel Jorgensen, Janet Warner, and the others whose names I do not know but whose contributions to my manuscript transformed it into this book, have enriched this collection with the deft skill and professionalism that has earned them and their publishing company the outstanding reputations all so richly deserve.

In the Beginning

In the beginning there was a Garden and a Palace. Twenty-two gates opened into the Garden. Twenty-two paths led from the gates to the Palace. But the Palace had only one door.

What an unusual palace it was! It was constructed with bricks that were crafted in the shapes of each of the twenty-two letters of the Hebrew *alef-bet.* The space between each letter and its neighbor was the mortar that held the Palace together.

The twenty-two gates to the Garden were each opened by a different key shaped like a dif-

3

ferent letter of the *alef-bet*. The *Alef* Gate would be opened only by the *alef* key, the *Bet* Gate only by the *bet* key, the *Gimel* Gate only by the *gimel* key.

In the Palace lived a King, Queen, Prince, and Princess.

4

The Sunbow

The sun rose early and stretched its rays across the sky. With its first stretch came deep red. With its next stretch came orange, and finally a golden glow sparkled everywhere.

Sometimes when the sun awakens, it is happy to have the world all to itself. There are other times, however, when it does not want to spend this precious time alone. So as it yawns and stretches, its rays reach through the windows and into the bedrooms of special children, warming them ever so gently until they twitch their

7

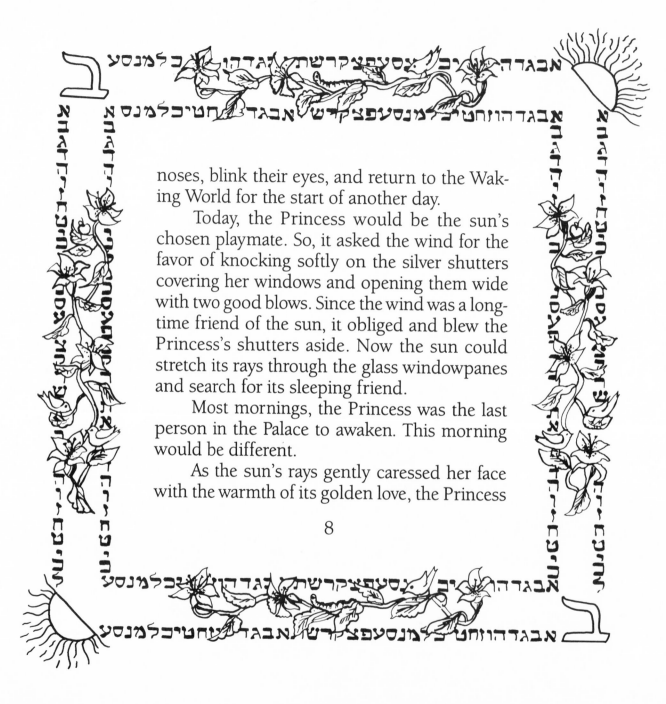

noses, blink their eyes, and return to the Waking World for the start of another day.

Today, the Princess would be the sun's chosen playmate. So, it asked the wind for the favor of knocking softly on the silver shutters covering her windows and opening them wide with two good blows. Since the wind was a long-time friend of the sun, it obliged and blew the Princess's shutters aside. Now the sun could stretch its rays through the glass windowpanes and search for its sleeping friend.

Most mornings, the Princess was the last person in the Palace to awaken. This morning would be different.

As the sun's rays gently caressed her face with the warmth of its golden love, the Princess

8

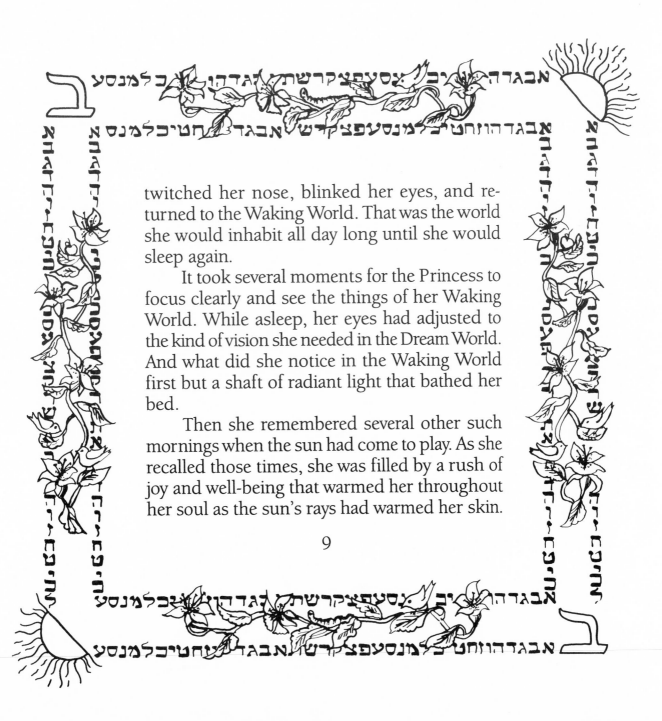

twitched her nose, blinked her eyes, and returned to the Waking World. That was the world she would inhabit all day long until she would sleep again.

It took several moments for the Princess to focus clearly and see the things of her Waking World. While asleep, her eyes had adjusted to the kind of vision she needed in the Dream World. And what did she notice in the Waking World first but a shaft of radiant light that bathed her bed.

Then she remembered several other such mornings when the sun had come to play. As she recalled those times, she was filled by a rush of joy and well-being that warmed her throughout her soul as the sun's rays had warmed her skin.

9

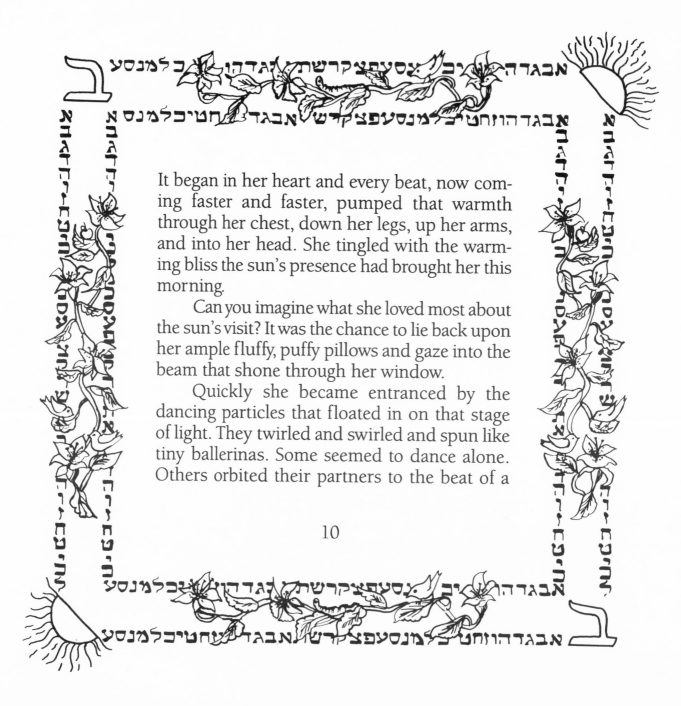

It began in her heart and every beat, now coming faster and faster, pumped that warmth
through her chest, down her legs, up her arms,
and into her head. She tingled with the warming bliss the sun's presence had brought her this
morning.

Can you imagine what she loved most about
the sun's visit? It was the chance to lie back upon
her ample fluffy, puffy pillows and gaze into the
beam that shone through her window.

Quickly she became entranced by the
dancing particles that floated in on that stage
of light. They twirled and swirled and spun like
tiny ballerinas. Some seemed to dance alone.
Others orbited their partners to the beat of a

10

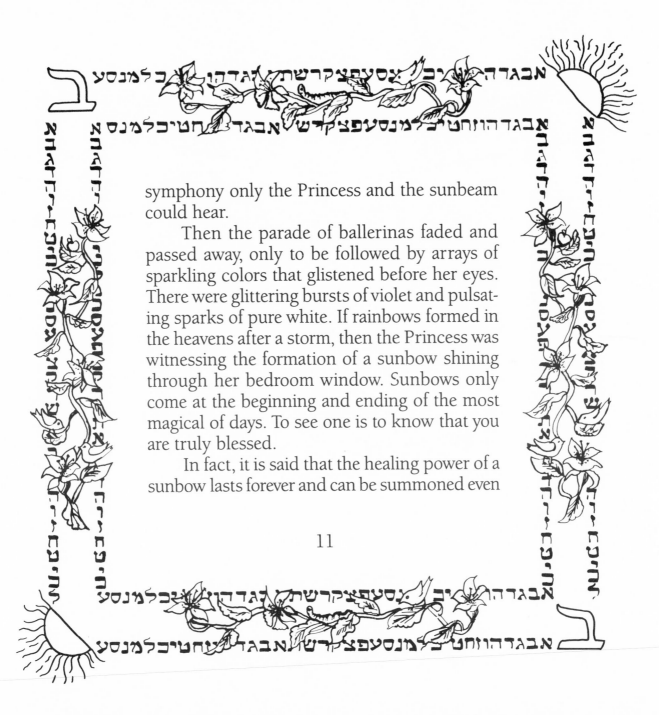

symphony only the Princess and the sunbeam could hear.

Then the parade of ballerinas faded and passed away, only to be followed by arrays of sparkling colors that glistened before her eyes. There were glittering bursts of violet and pulsating sparks of pure white. If rainbows formed in the heavens after a storm, then the Princess was witnessing the formation of a sunbow shining through her bedroom window. Sunbows only come at the beginning and ending of the most magical of days. To see one is to know that you are truly blessed.

In fact, it is said that the healing power of a sunbow lasts forever and can be summoned even

11

after many years have passed simply by recalling a time when one came to visit, no matter how
long ago that was.

And true to its blessing, the sunbow
brought the Princess a marvelous magical day.

12

The Gift in the Garden

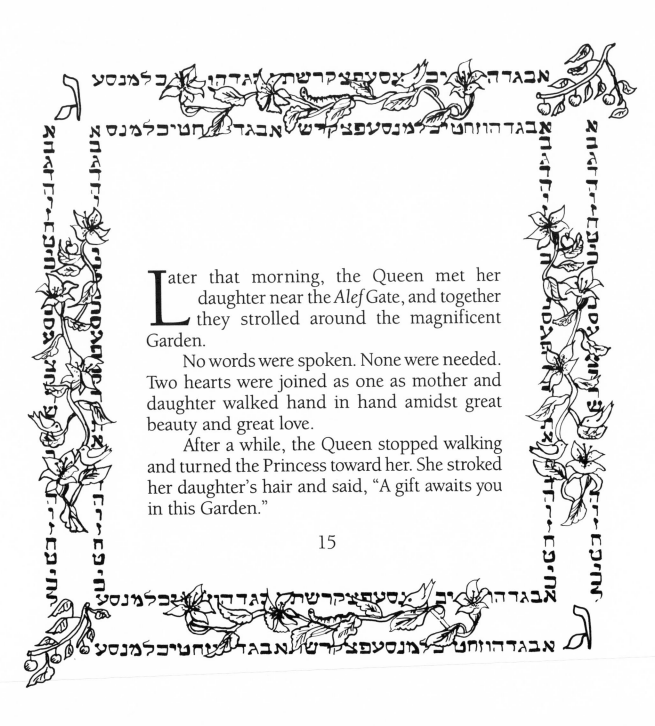

Later that morning, the Queen met her daughter near the *Alef* Gate, and together they strolled around the magnificent Garden.

No words were spoken. None were needed. Two hearts were joined as one as mother and daughter walked hand in hand amidst great beauty and great love.

After a while, the Queen stopped walking and turned the Princess toward her. She stroked her daughter's hair and said, "A gift awaits you in this Garden."

15

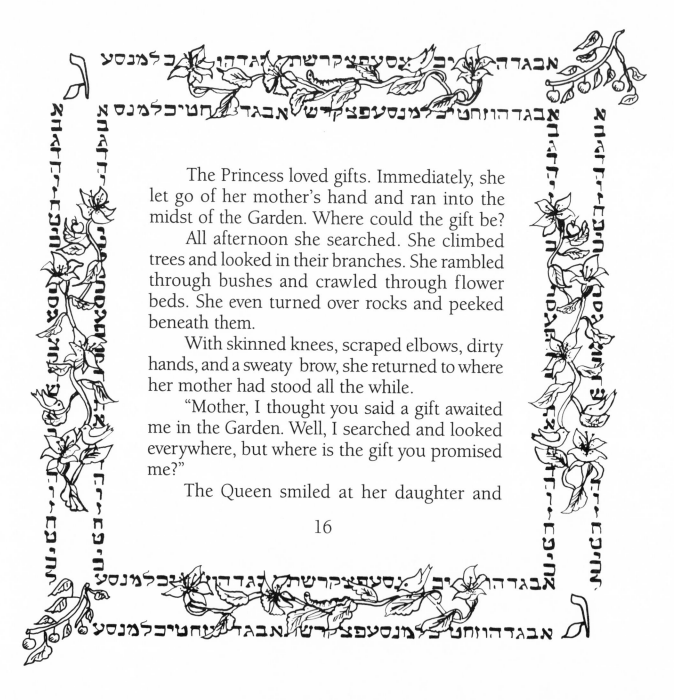

The Princess loved gifts. Immediately, she let go of her mother's hand and ran into the midst of the Garden. Where could the gift be?

All afternoon she searched. She climbed trees and looked in their branches. She rambled through bushes and crawled through flower beds. She even turned over rocks and peeked beneath them.

With skinned knees, scraped elbows, dirty hands, and a sweaty brow, she returned to where her mother had stood all the while.

"Mother, I thought you said a gift awaited me in the Garden. Well, I searched and looked everywhere, but where is the gift you promised me?"

The Queen smiled at her daughter and

16

touched her cheek. "Indeed, you found the gift I meant for you to find," she said. But her daughter was very confused. She did not think she had discovered anything at all.

When the Queen saw her daughter knit her brows in puzzlement, she explained, "Today you looked at your world very closely. You touched the world, and it seems as though the world touched you." Indeed, her daughter had grass stains on her skirt and smudges of dirt on her socks. She had twigs in her hair, and petals from assorted flowers of every color had fallen into the pockets of her blouse. Truly, everywhere she had searched, the world had left its mark on her.

"Today you explored the world carefully," the Queen continued. "You approached every

17

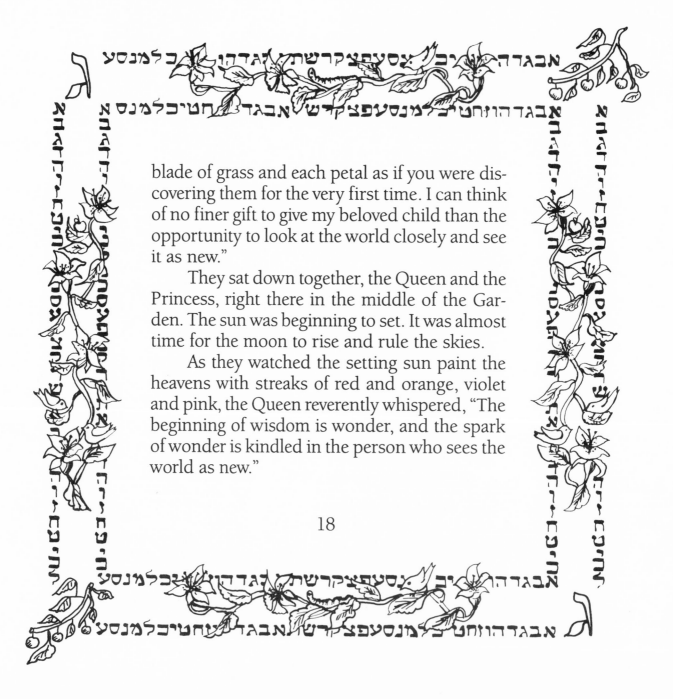

blade of grass and each petal as if you were discovering them for the very first time. I can think of no finer gift to give my beloved child than the opportunity to look at the world closely and see it as new."

They sat down together, the Queen and the Princess, right there in the middle of the Garden. The sun was beginning to set. It was almost time for the moon to rise and rule the skies.

As they watched the setting sun paint the heavens with streaks of red and orange, violet and pink, the Queen reverently whispered, "The beginning of wisdom is wonder, and the spark of wonder is kindled in the person who sees the world as new."

18

Light in the Darkness

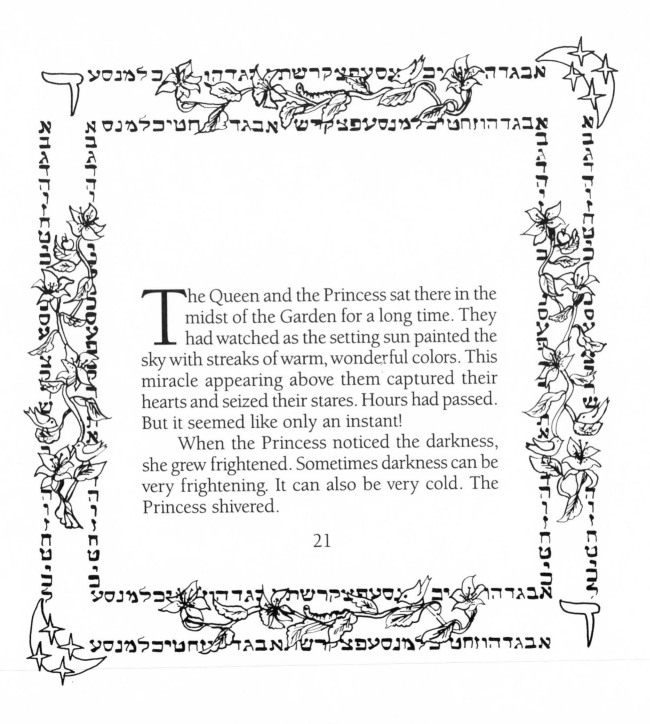

The Queen and the Princess sat there in the midst of the Garden for a long time. They had watched as the setting sun painted the sky with streaks of warm, wonderful colors. This miracle appearing above them captured their hearts and seized their stares. Hours had passed. But it seemed like only an instant!

When the Princess noticed the darkness, she grew frightened. Sometimes darkness can be very frightening. It can also be very cold. The Princess shivered.

21

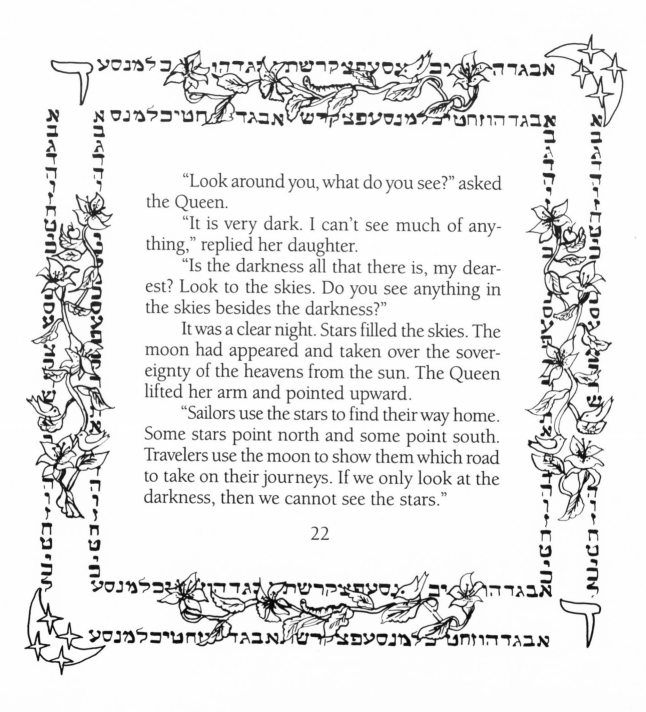

"Look around you, what do you see?" asked the Queen.

"It is very dark. I can't see much of anything," replied her daughter.

"Is the darkness all that there is, my dearest? Look to the skies. Do you see anything in the skies besides the darkness?"

It was a clear night. Stars filled the skies. The moon had appeared and taken over the sovereignty of the heavens from the sun. The Queen lifted her arm and pointed upward.

"Sailors use the stars to find their way home. Some stars point north and some point south. Travelers use the moon to show them which road to take on their journeys. If we only look at the darkness, then we cannot see the stars."

22

The Queen explained to her daughter that there is some light in any darkness. We simply have to look for it.

"In fact," she said, "there is even a star called *Mazal*. It brings good fortune to any who find it."

"Where is it, Mother?" asked the Princess. "Which star is the one called *Mazal*?"

"It is always the one that sparkles most," replied the Queen. "Tonight, where do you think it is?"

The Princess searched the heavens. "There it is," she proclaimed. "There is the *Mazal* star."

"There it is," agreed the Queen. "Shall we go inside now?"

"Oh, no, Mother," pleaded the Princess. "I want to look at the *Mazal* star a bit longer."

23

"But I thought the darkness frightened you," said the Queen.

"Not when I am looking at the *Mazal* star. Then I see only the light," said the Princess.

And the Queen and the Princess sat and gazed upon the *Mazal* star a good long time.

24

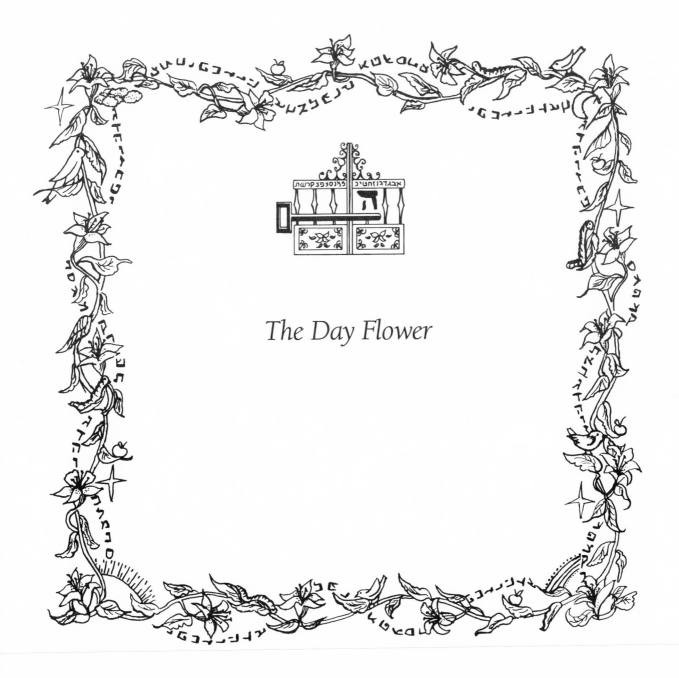

The Day Flower

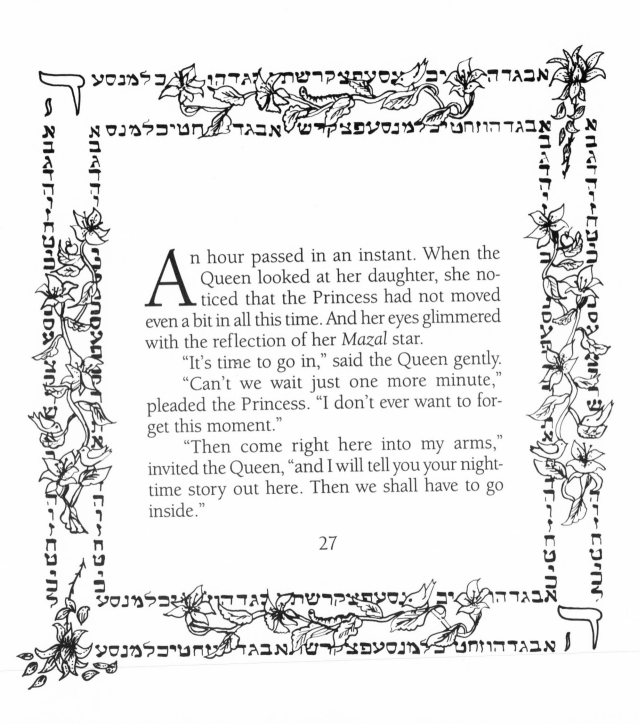

An hour passed in an instant. When the Queen looked at her daughter, she noticed that the Princess had not moved even a bit in all this time. And her eyes glimmered with the reflection of her *Mazal* star.

"It's time to go in," said the Queen gently.

"Can't we wait just one more minute," pleaded the Princess. "I don't ever want to forget this moment."

"Then come right here into my arms," invited the Queen, "and I will tell you your nighttime story out here. Then we shall have to go inside."

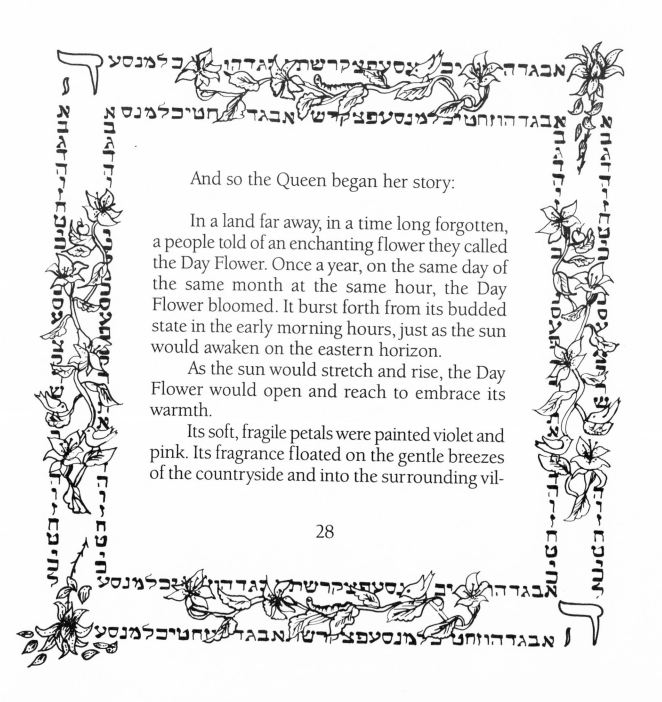

And so the Queen began her story:

In a land far away, in a time long forgotten, a people told of an enchanting flower they called the Day Flower. Once a year, on the same day of the same month at the same hour, the Day Flower bloomed. It burst forth from its budded state in the early morning hours, just as the sun would awaken on the eastern horizon.

As the sun would stretch and rise, the Day Flower would open and reach to embrace its warmth.

Its soft, fragile petals were painted violet and pink. Its fragrance floated on the gentle breezes of the countryside and into the surrounding vil-

28

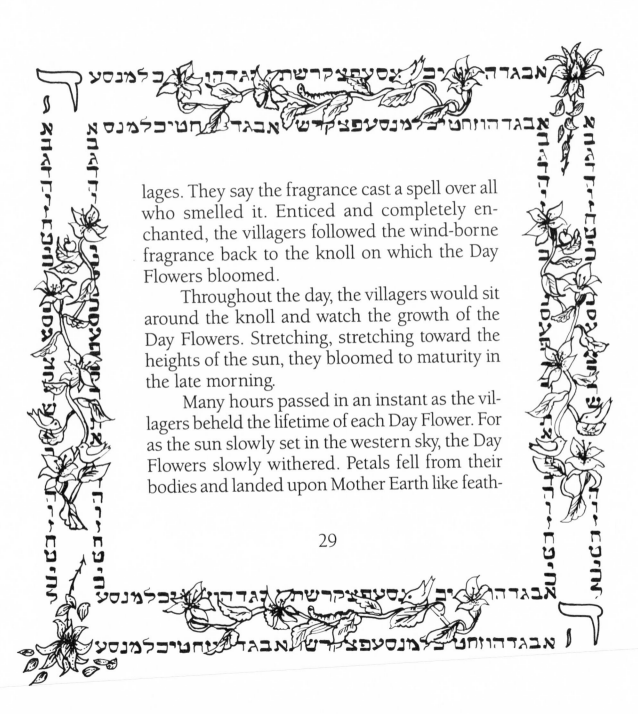

lages. They say the fragrance cast a spell over all who smelled it. Enticed and completely enchanted, the villagers followed the wind-borne fragrance back to the knoll on which the Day Flowers bloomed.

Throughout the day, the villagers would sit around the knoll and watch the growth of the Day Flowers. Stretching, stretching toward the heights of the sun, they bloomed to maturity in the late morning.

Many hours passed in an instant as the villagers beheld the lifetime of each Day Flower. For as the sun slowly set in the western sky, the Day Flowers slowly withered. Petals fell from their bodies and landed upon Mother Earth like feath-

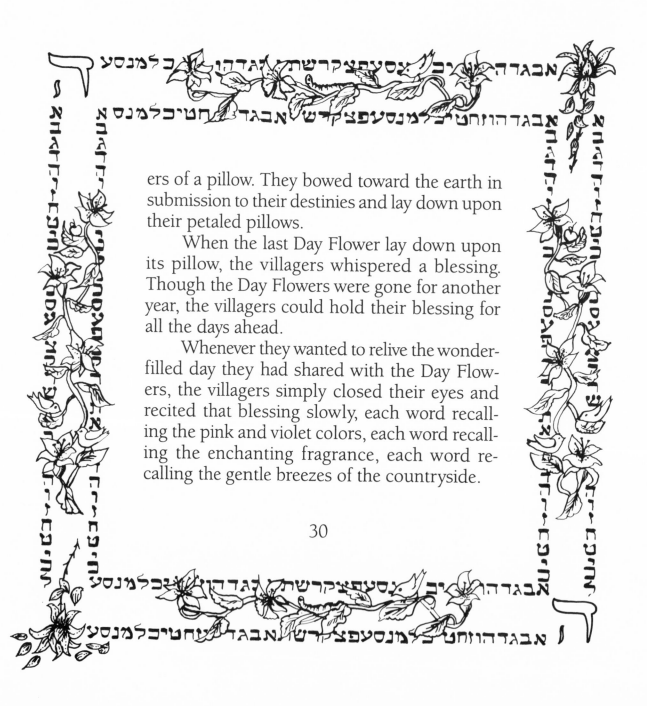

ers of a pillow. They bowed toward the earth in submission to their destinies and lay down upon their petaled pillows.

When the last Day Flower lay down upon its pillow, the villagers whispered a blessing. Though the Day Flowers were gone for another year, the villagers could hold their blessing for all the days ahead.

Whenever they wanted to relive the wonder-filled day they had shared with the Day Flowers, the villagers simply closed their eyes and recited that blessing slowly, each word recalling the pink and violet colors, each word recalling the enchanting fragrance, each word recalling the gentle breezes of the countryside.

30

"Shall we say a blessing to imprint this night on our hearts forever?" asked the Queen.

The Princess nodded.

"What blessing would you like to say?"

The Princess closed her eyes and recalled this beautiful night with her mother. She recalled the sparkle of her *Mazal* star. She recalled the pale glow of the full moon. She recalled the soft black sky that now felt like a safe, soft blanket. She recalled the touch of her mother's embrace, the fragrance of her mother's hair, and the love in her mother's voice.

And then she recited a blessing that would hold these moments for her forever.

31

Finding a Balance

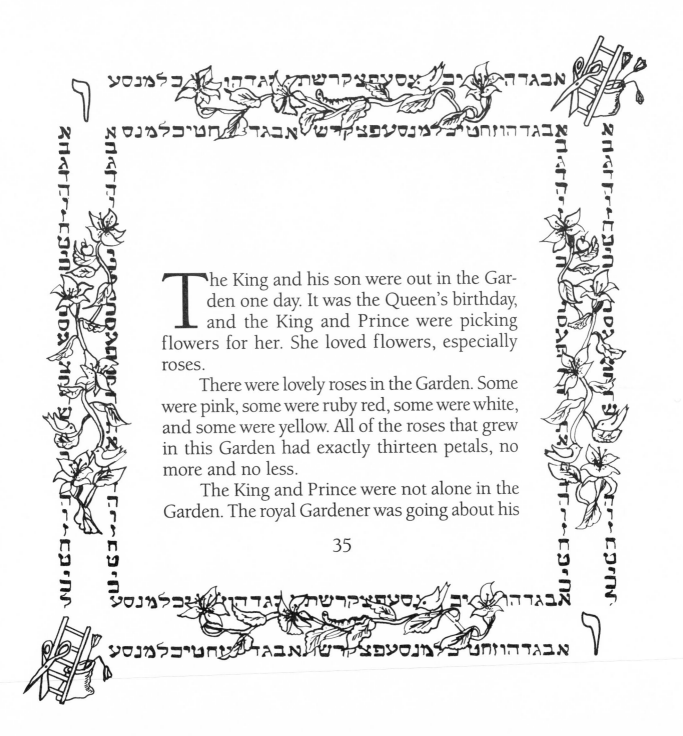

The King and his son were out in the Garden one day. It was the Queen's birthday, and the King and Prince were picking flowers for her. She loved flowers, especially roses.

There were lovely roses in the Garden. Some were pink, some were ruby red, some were white, and some were yellow. All of the roses that grew in this Garden had exactly thirteen petals, no more and no less.

The King and Prince were not alone in the Garden. The royal Gardener was going about his

35

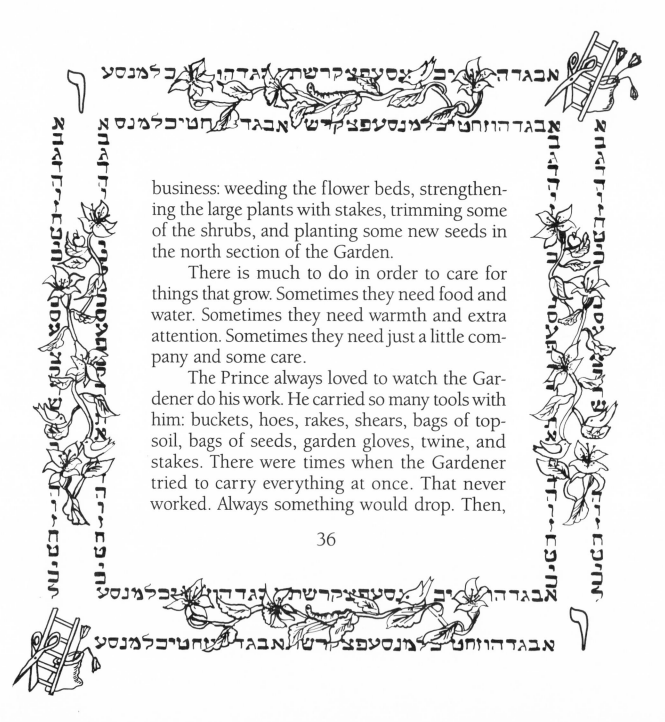

business: weeding the flower beds, strengthening the large plants with stakes, trimming some of the shrubs, and planting some new seeds in the north section of the Garden.

There is much to do in order to care for things that grow. Sometimes they need food and water. Sometimes they need warmth and extra attention. Sometimes they need just a little company and some care.

The Prince always loved to watch the Gardener do his work. He carried so many tools with him: buckets, hoes, rakes, shears, bags of topsoil, bags of seeds, garden gloves, twine, and stakes. There were times when the Gardener tried to carry everything at once. That never worked. Always something would drop. Then,

36

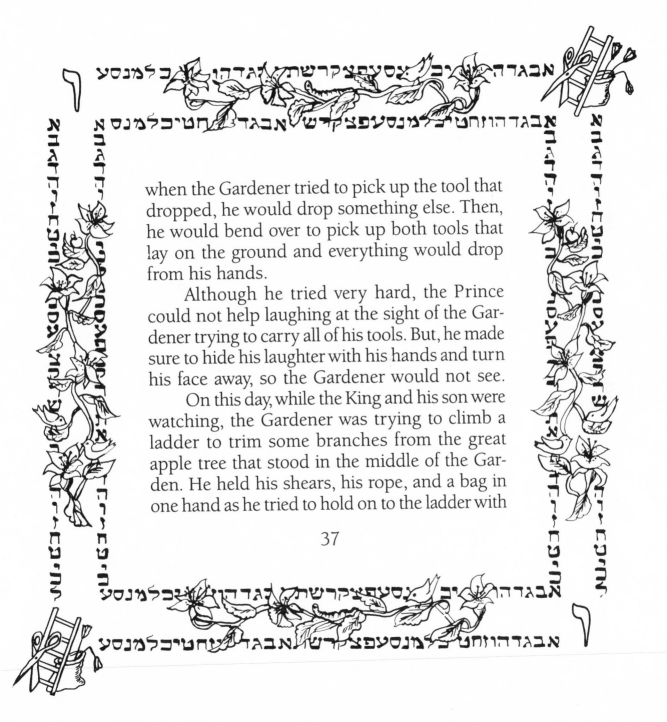

when the Gardener tried to pick up the tool that dropped, he would drop something else. Then, he would bend over to pick up both tools that lay on the ground and everything would drop from his hands.

Although he tried very hard, the Prince could not help laughing at the sight of the Gardener trying to carry all of his tools. But, he made sure to hide his laughter with his hands and turn his face away, so the Gardener would not see.

On this day, while the King and his son were watching, the Gardener was trying to climb a ladder to trim some branches from the great apple tree that stood in the middle of the Garden. He held his shears, his rope, and a bag in one hand as he tried to hold on to the ladder with

37

his other hand. The poor Gardener took one step up the ladder. Unfortunately, he was holding so much in his right hand that he began to lean to that side. Losing his balance, he fell to the ground.

So, to solve his problem, the Gardener switched his tools to his left hand and grabbed for the ladder with his free right hand. This time, he began to sway to his left and lost his balance again. For a second time he fell to the ground. Luckily, he had taken only the first step up the ladder and did not fall very far.

The King turned to his son and asked him, "What seems to be our Gardener's problem?"

The Prince did not think very long. He smiled as though he immediately knew the

answer to his father's question. "Our Gardener is clumsy," the Prince blurted out with great expectation for approval.

Instead, the King shook his head no and patiently observed, "All you have done is insult our fine friend, the Gardener. You have not noticed the heart of his problem." Then he asked the Prince to think about it again.

So, the Prince thought some more. Once again, he smiled as he responded. This time he was sure that he was about to get to the heart of the Gardener's problem. "The Gardener is carrying too many tools," he said.

Again, the King shook his head and patiently observed, "We can always carry more than we think we can, if . . ."

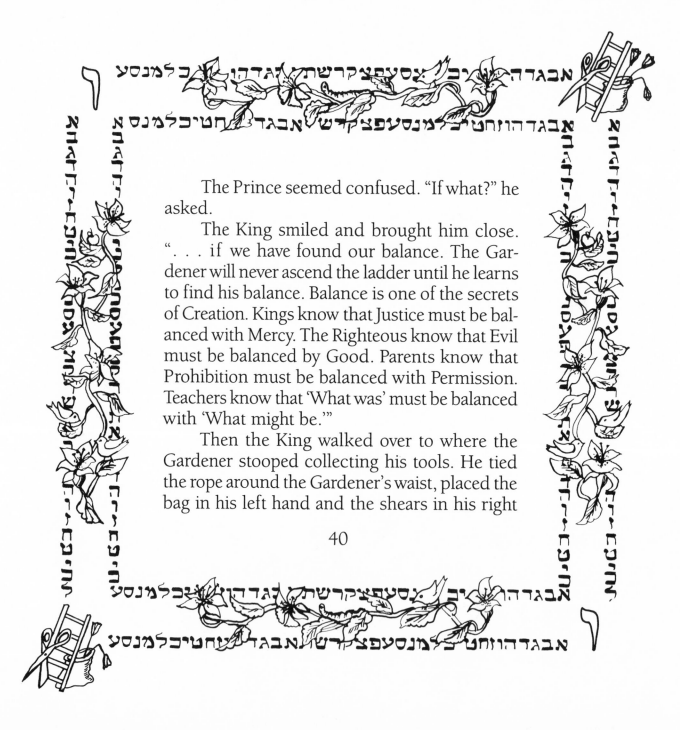

The Prince seemed confused. "If what?" he asked.

The King smiled and brought him close. ". . . if we have found our balance. The Gardener will never ascend the ladder until he learns to find his balance. Balance is one of the secrets of Creation. Kings know that Justice must be balanced with Mercy. The Righteous know that Evil must be balanced by Good. Parents know that Prohibition must be balanced with Permission. Teachers know that 'What was' must be balanced with 'What might be.'"

Then the King walked over to where the Gardener stooped collecting his tools. He tied the rope around the Gardener's waist, placed the bag in his left hand and the shears in his right

40

hand. In moments, the Gardener had climbed to the top of the ladder and began pruning the apple tree.

"Balance," said the King to his son. "It's one of the greatest of all the secrets of the universe."

You Must See for Yourself

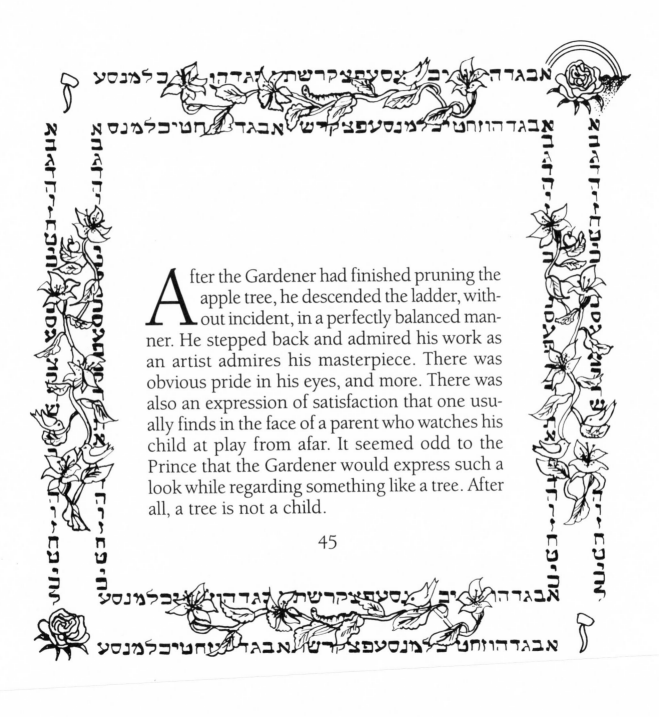

After the Gardener had finished pruning the apple tree, he descended the ladder, without incident, in a perfectly balanced manner. He stepped back and admired his work as an artist admires his masterpiece. There was obvious pride in his eyes, and more. There was also an expression of satisfaction that one usually finds in the face of a parent who watches his child at play from afar. It seemed odd to the Prince that the Gardener would express such a look while regarding something like a tree. After all, a tree is not a child.

45

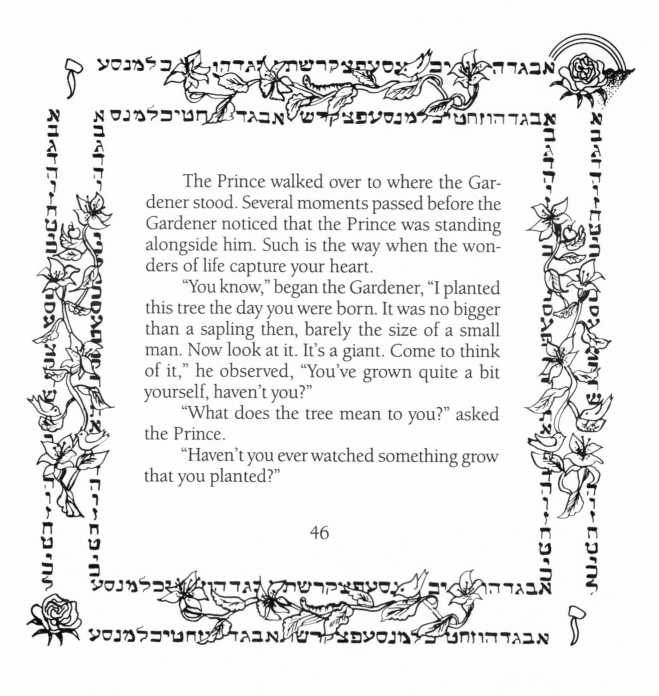

The Prince walked over to where the Gardener stood. Several moments passed before the Gardener noticed that the Prince was standing alongside him. Such is the way when the wonders of life capture your heart.

"You know," began the Gardener, "I planted this tree the day you were born. It was no bigger than a sapling then, barely the size of a small man. Now look at it. It's a giant. Come to think of it," he observed, "You've grown quite a bit yourself, haven't you?"

"What does the tree mean to you?" asked the Prince.

"Haven't you ever watched something grow that you planted?"

46

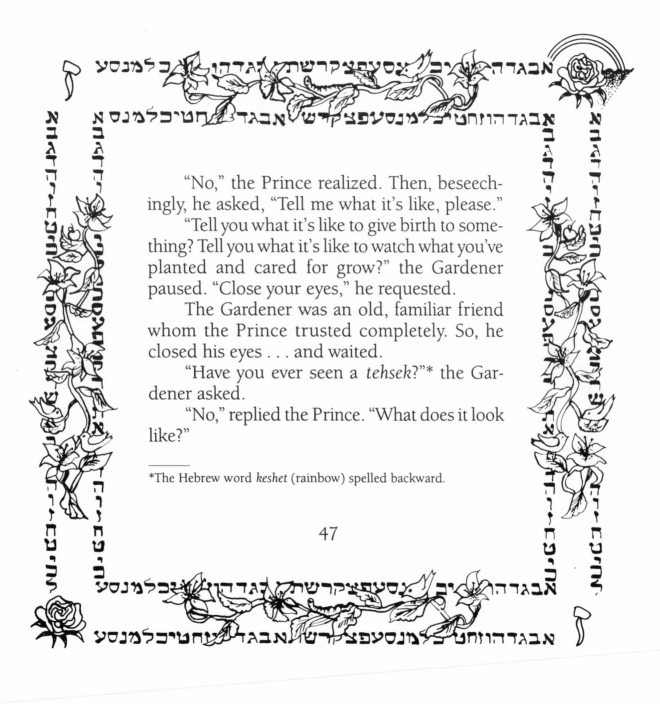

"No," the Prince realized. Then, beseechingly, he asked, "Tell me what it's like, please."

"Tell you what it's like to give birth to something? Tell you what it's like to watch what you've planted and cared for grow?" the Gardener paused. "Close your eyes," he requested.

The Gardener was an old, familiar friend whom the Prince trusted completely. So, he closed his eyes . . . and waited.

"Have you ever seen a *tehsek*?"* the Gardener asked.

"No," replied the Prince. "What does it look like?"

---

*The Hebrew word *keshet* (rainbow) spelled backward.

47

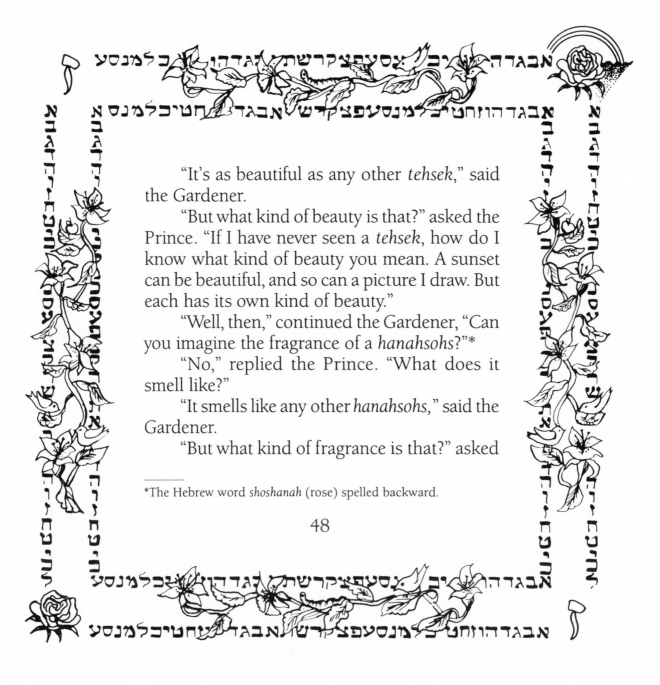

"It's as beautiful as any other *tehsek*," said the Gardener.

"But what kind of beauty is that?" asked the Prince. "If I have never seen a *tehsek*, how do I know what kind of beauty you mean. A sunset can be beautiful, and so can a picture I draw. But each has its own kind of beauty."

"Well, then," continued the Gardener, "Can you imagine the fragrance of a *hanahsohs*?"*

"No," replied the Prince. "What does it smell like?"

"It smells like any other *hanahsohs,*" said the Gardener.

"But what kind of fragrance is that?" asked

---

*The Hebrew word *shoshanah* (rose) spelled backward.

48

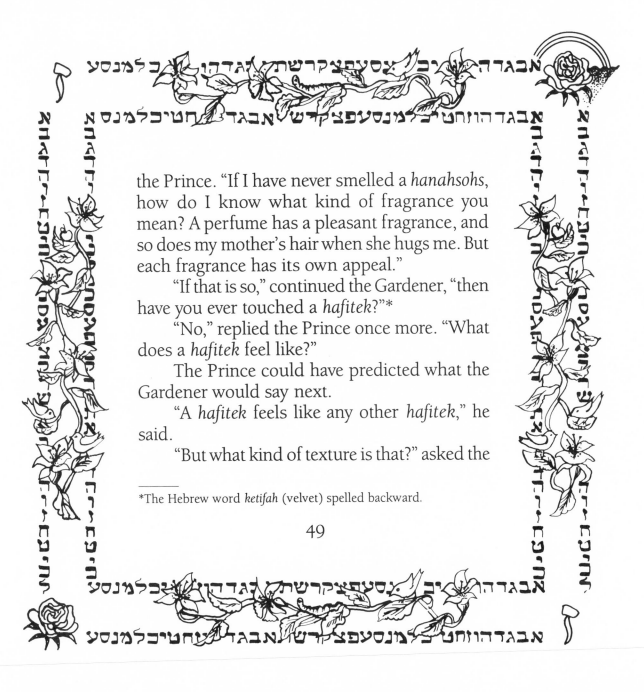

the Prince. "If I have never smelled a *hanahsohs*, how do I know what kind of fragrance you mean? A perfume has a pleasant fragrance, and so does my mother's hair when she hugs me. But each fragrance has its own appeal."

"If that is so," continued the Gardener, "then have you ever touched a *hafitek*?"*

"No," replied the Prince once more. "What does a *hafitek* feel like?"

The Prince could have predicted what the Gardener would say next.

"A *hafitek* feels like any other *hafitek*," he said.

"But what kind of texture is that?" asked the

---

*The Hebrew word *ketifah* (velvet) spelled backward.

49

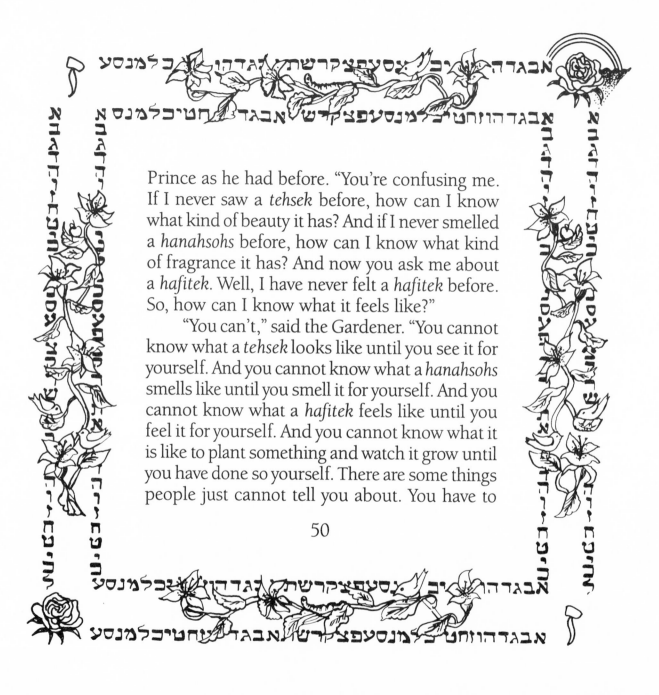

Prince as he had before. "You're confusing me. If I never saw a *tehsek* before, how can I know what kind of beauty it has? And if I never smelled a *hanahsohs* before, how can I know what kind of fragrance it has? And now you ask me about a *hafitek*. Well, I have never felt a *hafitek* before. So, how can I know what it feels like?"

"You can't," said the Gardener. "You cannot know what a *tehsek* looks like until you see it for yourself. And you cannot know what a *hanahsohs* smells like until you smell it for yourself. And you cannot know what a *hafitek* feels like until you feel it for yourself. And you cannot know what it is like to plant something and watch it grow until you have done so yourself. There are some things people just cannot tell you about. You have to

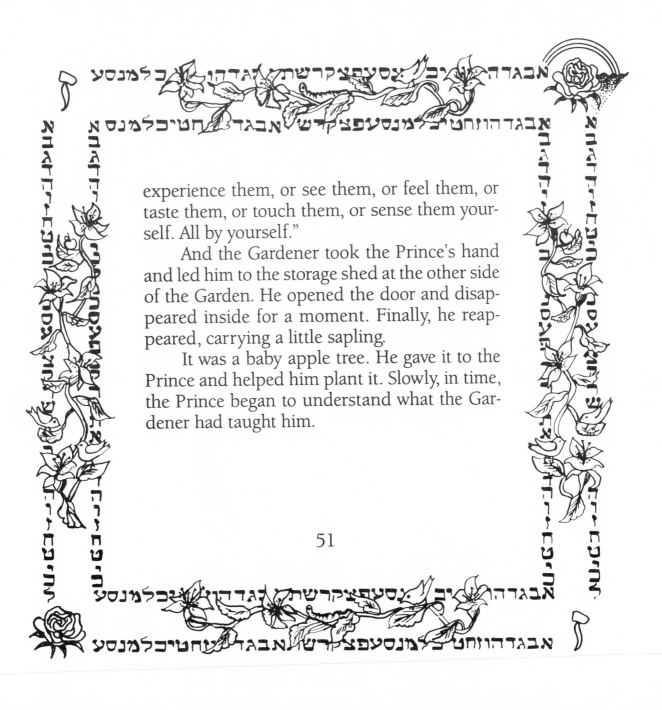

experience them, or see them, or feel them, or taste them, or touch them, or sense them yourself. All by yourself."

And the Gardener took the Prince's hand and led him to the storage shed at the other side of the Garden. He opened the door and disappeared inside for a moment. Finally, he reappeared, carrying a little sapling.

It was a baby apple tree. He gave it to the Prince and helped him plant it. Slowly, in time, the Prince began to understand what the Gardener had taught him.

A Bedtime Story

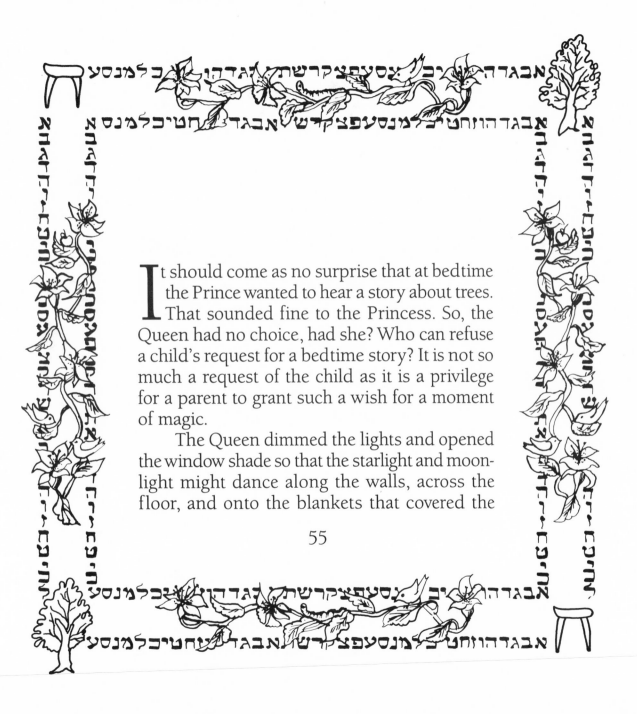

It should come as no surprise that at bedtime the Prince wanted to hear a story about trees. That sounded fine to the Princess. So, the Queen had no choice, had she? Who can refuse a child's request for a bedtime story? It is not so much a request of the child as it is a privilege for a parent to grant such a wish for a moment of magic.

The Queen dimmed the lights and opened the window shade so that the starlight and moonlight might dance along the walls, across the floor, and onto the blankets that covered the

55

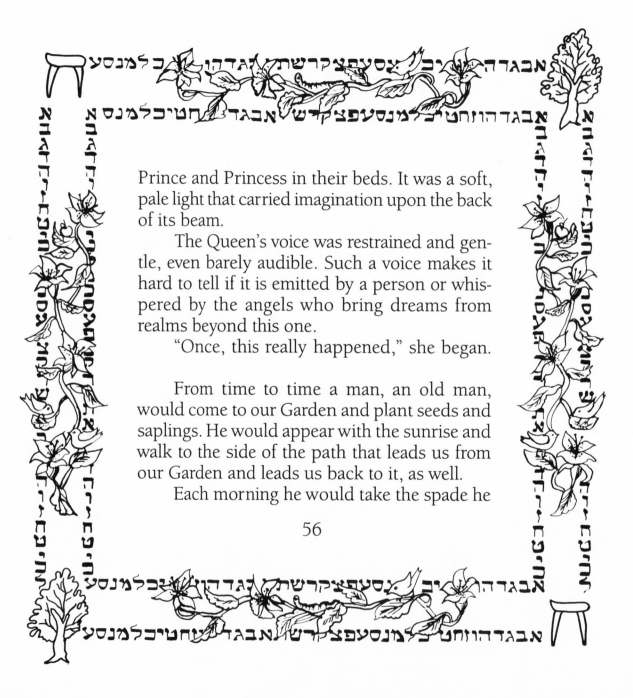

Prince and Princess in their beds. It was a soft, pale light that carried imagination upon the back of its beam.

The Queen's voice was restrained and gentle, even barely audible. Such a voice makes it hard to tell if it is emitted by a person or whispered by the angels who bring dreams from realms beyond this one.

"Once, this really happened," she began.

From time to time a man, an old man, would come to our Garden and plant seeds and saplings. He would appear with the sunrise and walk to the side of the path that leads us from our Garden and leads us back to it, as well.

Each morning he would take the spade he

56

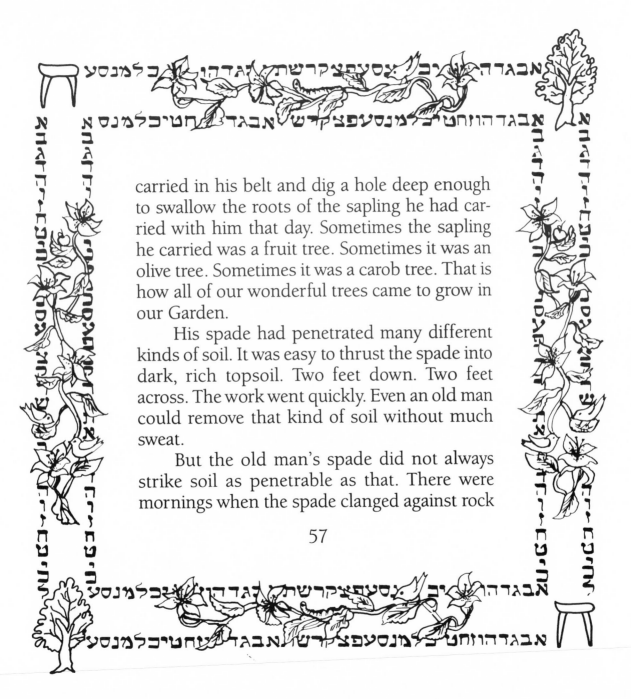

carried in his belt and dig a hole deep enough to swallow the roots of the sapling he had carried with him that day. Sometimes the sapling he carried was a fruit tree. Sometimes it was an olive tree. Sometimes it was a carob tree. That is how all of our wonderful trees came to grow in our Garden.

His spade had penetrated many different kinds of soil. It was easy to thrust the spade into dark, rich topsoil. Two feet down. Two feet across. The work went quickly. Even an old man could remove that kind of soil without much sweat.

But the old man's spade did not always strike soil as penetrable as that. There were mornings when the spade clanged against rock

57

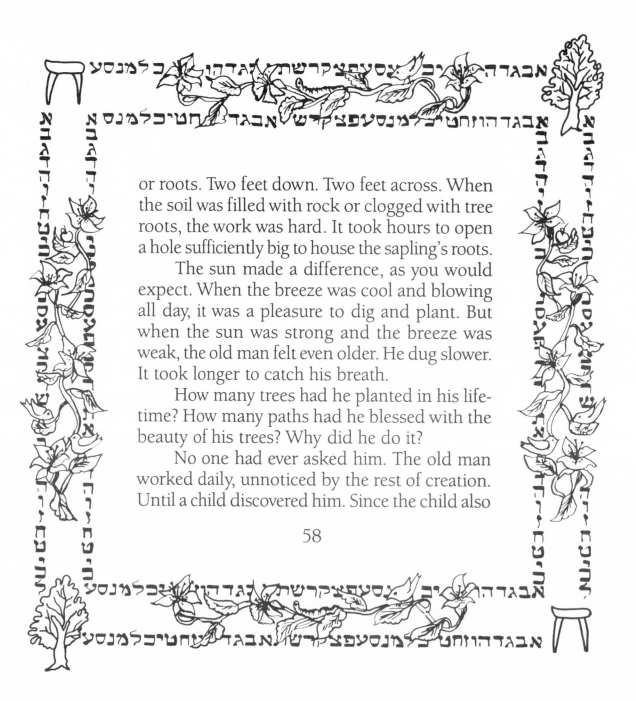

or roots. Two feet down. Two feet across. When the soil was filled with rock or clogged with tree roots, the work was hard. It took hours to open a hole sufficiently big to house the sapling's roots.

The sun made a difference, as you would expect. When the breeze was cool and blowing all day, it was a pleasure to dig and plant. But when the sun was strong and the breeze was weak, the old man felt even older. He dug slower. It took longer to catch his breath.

How many trees had he planted in his lifetime? How many paths had he blessed with the beauty of his trees? Why did he do it?

No one had ever asked him. The old man worked daily, unnoticed by the rest of creation. Until a child discovered him. Since the child also

58

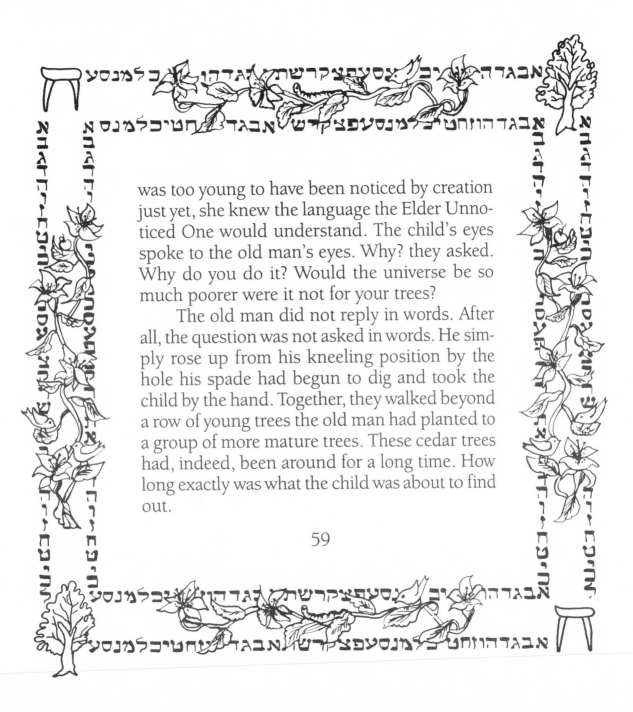

was too young to have been noticed by creation just yet, she knew the language the Elder Unnoticed One would understand. The child's eyes spoke to the old man's eyes. Why? they asked. Why do you do it? Would the universe be so much poorer were it not for your trees?

The old man did not reply in words. After all, the question was not asked in words. He simply rose up from his kneeling position by the hole his spade had begun to dig and took the child by the hand. Together, they walked beyond a row of young trees the old man had planted to a group of more mature trees. These cedar trees had, indeed, been around for a long time. How long exactly was what the child was about to find out.

59

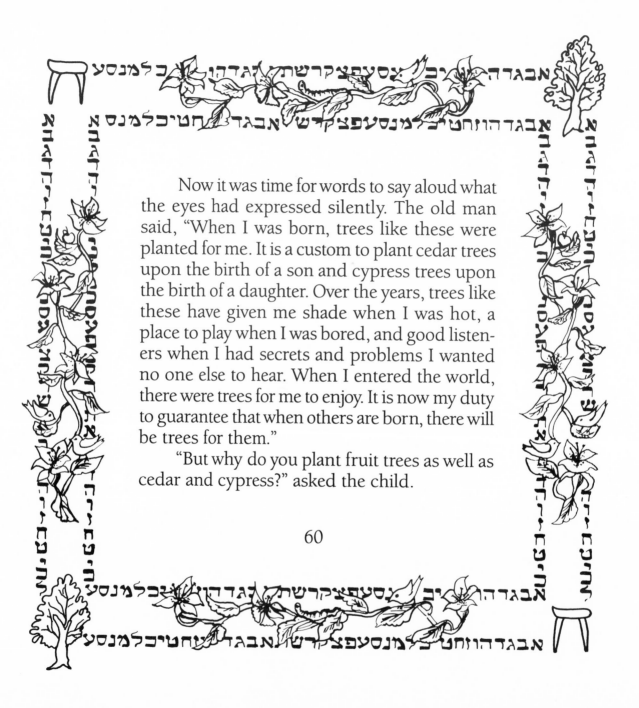

Now it was time for words to say aloud what the eyes had expressed silently. The old man said, "When I was born, trees like these were planted for me. It is a custom to plant cedar trees upon the birth of a son and cypress trees upon the birth of a daughter. Over the years, trees like these have given me shade when I was hot, a place to play when I was bored, and good listeners when I had secrets and problems I wanted no one else to hear. When I entered the world, there were trees for me to enjoy. It is now my duty to guarantee that when others are born, there will be trees for them."

"But why do you plant fruit trees as well as cedar and cypress?" asked the child.

60

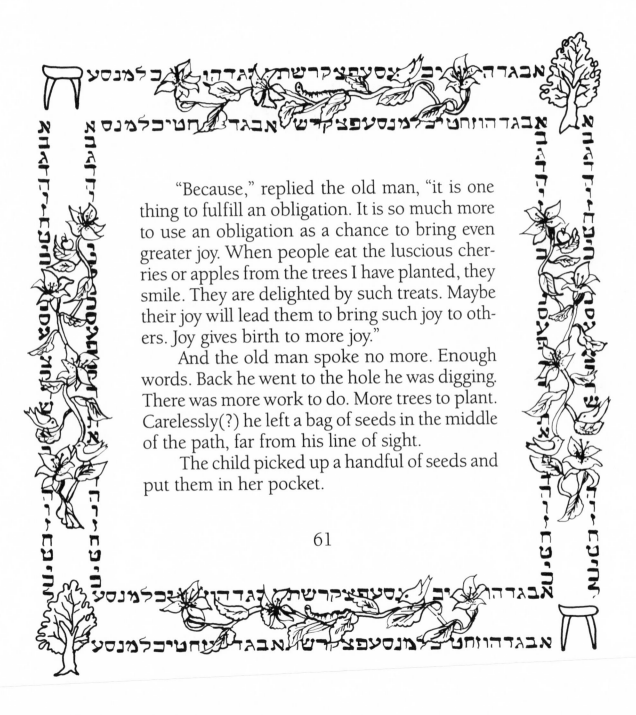

"Because," replied the old man, "it is one thing to fulfill an obligation. It is so much more to use an obligation as a chance to bring even greater joy. When people eat the luscious cherries or apples from the trees I have planted, they smile. They are delighted by such treats. Maybe their joy will lead them to bring such joy to others. Joy gives birth to more joy."

And the old man spoke no more. Enough words. Back he went to the hole he was digging. There was more work to do. More trees to plant. Carelessly(?) he left a bag of seeds in the middle of the path, far from his line of sight.

The child picked up a handful of seeds and put them in her pocket.

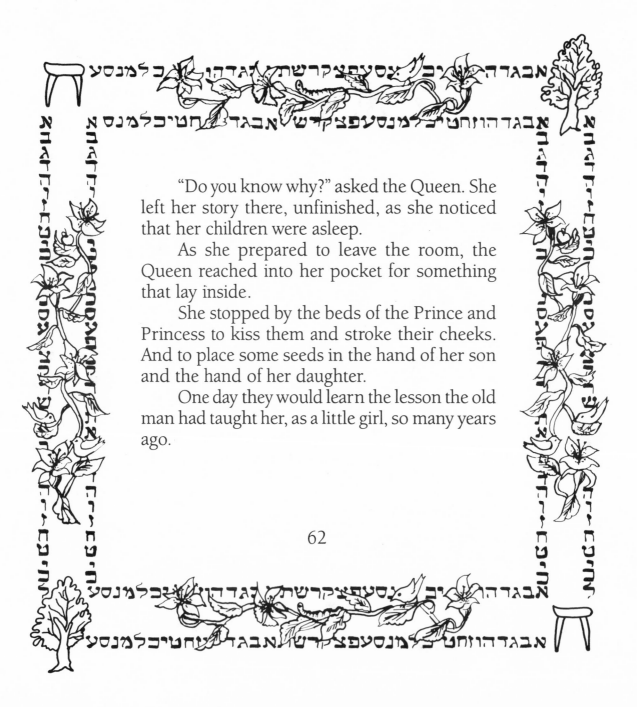

"Do you know why?" asked the Queen. She left her story there, unfinished, as she noticed that her children were asleep.

As she prepared to leave the room, the Queen reached into her pocket for something that lay inside.

She stopped by the beds of the Prince and Princess to kiss them and stroke their cheeks. And to place some seeds in the hand of her son and the hand of her daughter.

One day they would learn the lesson the old man had taught her, as a little girl, so many years ago.

*If You Think
You Are a Chicken*

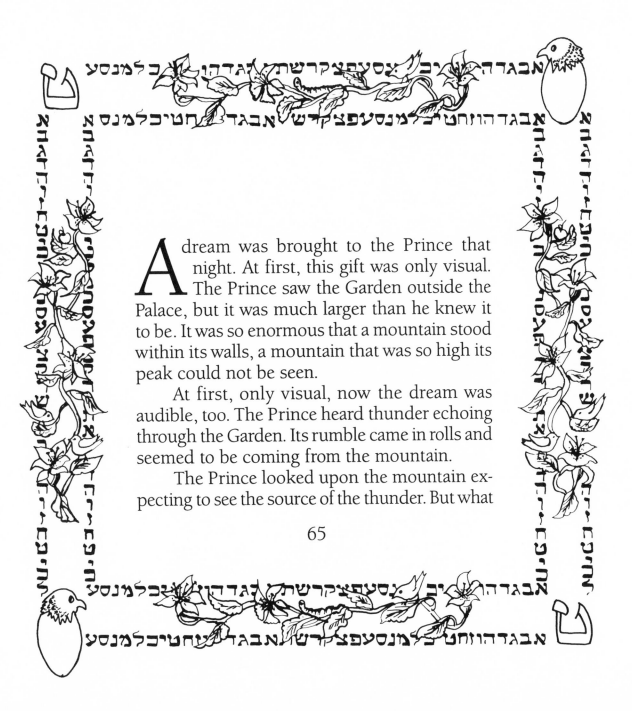

A dream was brought to the Prince that night. At first, this gift was only visual. The Prince saw the Garden outside the Palace, but it was much larger than he knew it to be. It was so enormous that a mountain stood within its walls, a mountain that was so high its peak could not be seen.

At first, only visual, now the dream was audible, too. The Prince heard thunder echoing through the Garden. Its rumble came in rolls and seemed to be coming from the mountain.

The Prince looked upon the mountain expecting to see the source of the thunder. But what

65

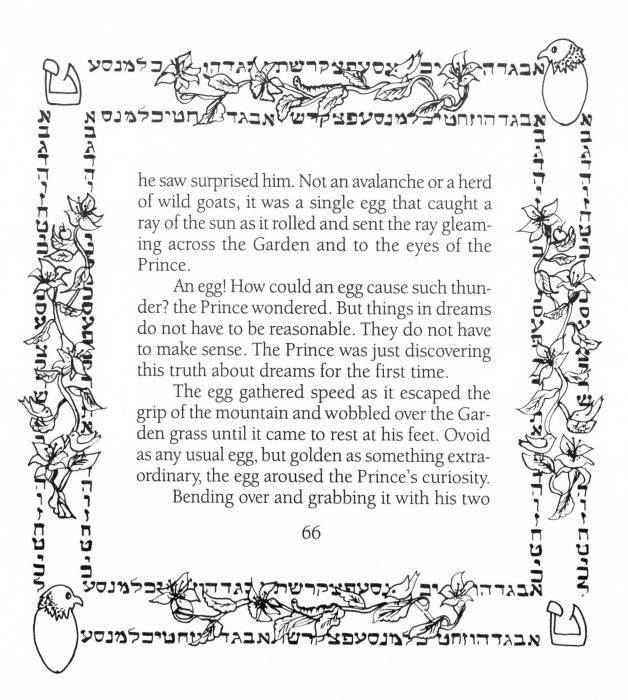

he saw surprised him. Not an avalanche or a herd of wild goats, it was a single egg that caught a ray of the sun as it rolled and sent the ray gleaming across the Garden and to the eyes of the Prince.

An egg! How could an egg cause such thunder? the Prince wondered. But things in dreams do not have to be reasonable. They do not have to make sense. The Prince was just discovering this truth about dreams for the first time.

The egg gathered speed as it escaped the grip of the mountain and wobbled over the Garden grass until it came to rest at his feet. Ovoid as any usual egg, but golden as something extraordinary, the egg aroused the Prince's curiosity.

Bending over and grabbing it with his two

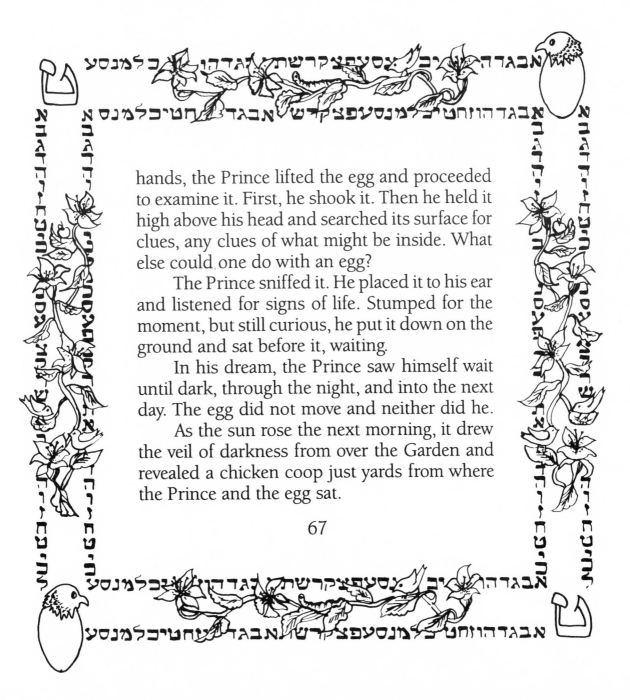

hands, the Prince lifted the egg and proceeded to examine it. First, he shook it. Then he held it high above his head and searched its surface for clues, any clues of what might be inside. What else could one do with an egg?

The Prince sniffed it. He placed it to his ear and listened for signs of life. Stumped for the moment, but still curious, he put it down on the ground and sat before it, waiting.

In his dream, the Prince saw himself wait until dark, through the night, and into the next day. The egg did not move and neither did he.

As the sun rose the next morning, it drew the veil of darkness from over the Garden and revealed a chicken coop just yards from where the Prince and the egg sat.

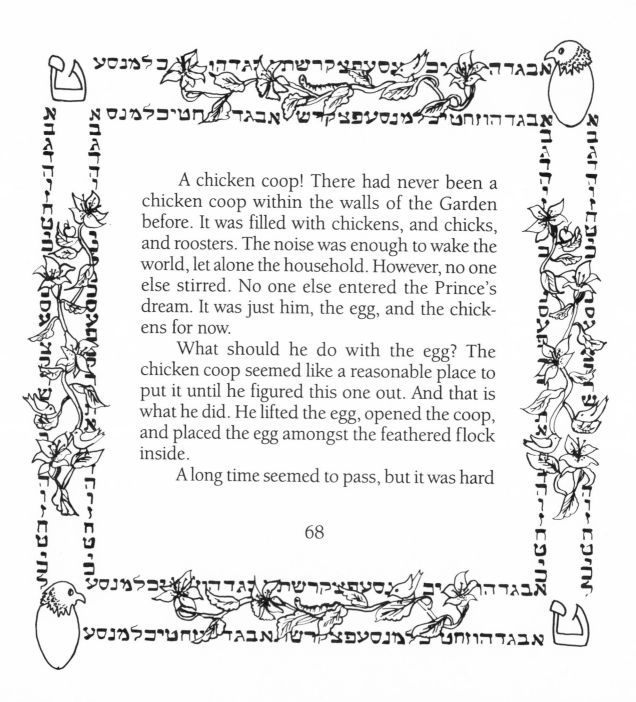

A chicken coop! There had never been a chicken coop within the walls of the Garden before. It was filled with chickens, and chicks, and roosters. The noise was enough to wake the world, let alone the household. However, no one else stirred. No one else entered the Prince's dream. It was just him, the egg, and the chickens for now.

What should he do with the egg? The chicken coop seemed like a reasonable place to put it until he figured this one out. And that is what he did. He lifted the egg, opened the coop, and placed the egg amongst the feathered flock inside.

A long time seemed to pass, but it was hard

68

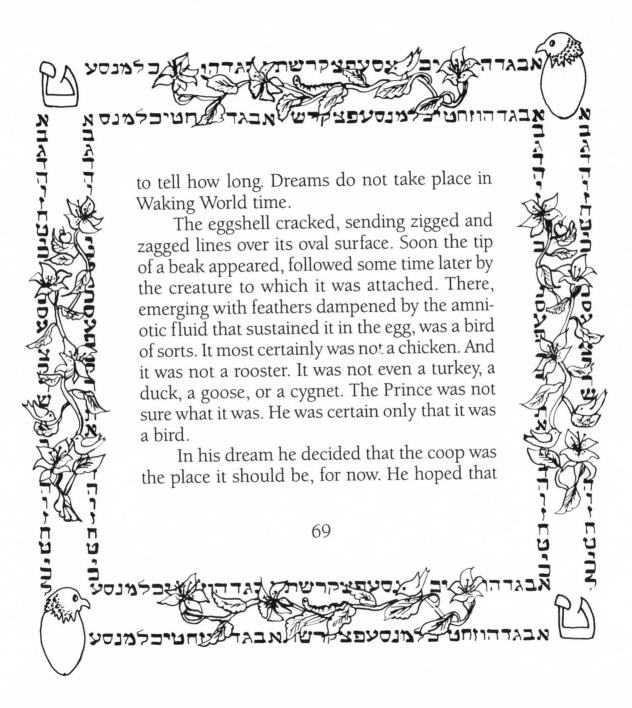

to tell how long. Dreams do not take place in Waking World time.

The eggshell cracked, sending zigged and zagged lines over its oval surface. Soon the tip of a beak appeared, followed some time later by the creature to which it was attached. There, emerging with feathers dampened by the amniotic fluid that sustained it in the egg, was a bird of sorts. It most certainly was not a chicken. And it was not a rooster. It was not even a turkey, a duck, a goose, or a cygnet. The Prince was not sure what it was. He was certain only that it was a bird.

In his dream he decided that the coop was the place it should be, for now. He hoped that

69

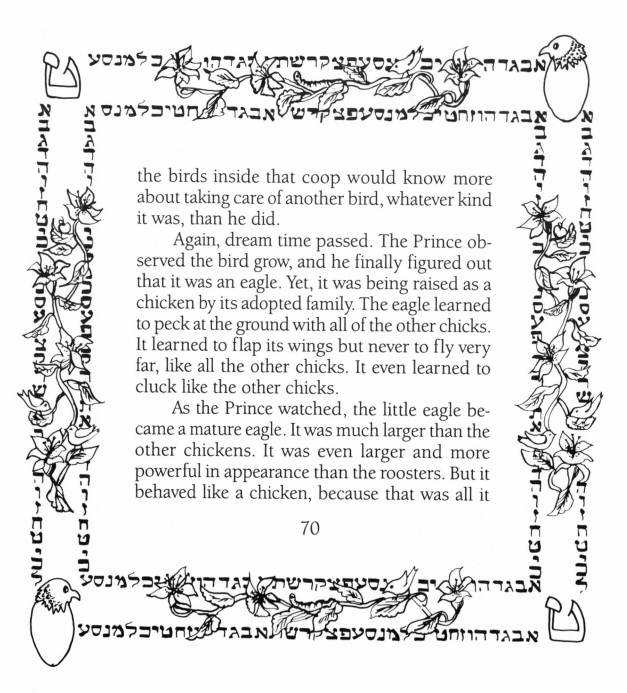

the birds inside that coop would know more about taking care of another bird, whatever kind it was, than he did.

Again, dream time passed. The Prince observed the bird grow, and he finally figured out that it was an eagle. Yet, it was being raised as a chicken by its adopted family. The eagle learned to peck at the ground with all of the other chicks. It learned to flap its wings but never to fly very far, like all the other chicks. It even learned to cluck like the other chicks.

As the Prince watched, the little eagle became a mature eagle. It was much larger than the other chickens. It was even larger and more powerful in appearance than the roosters. But it behaved like a chicken, because that was all it

70

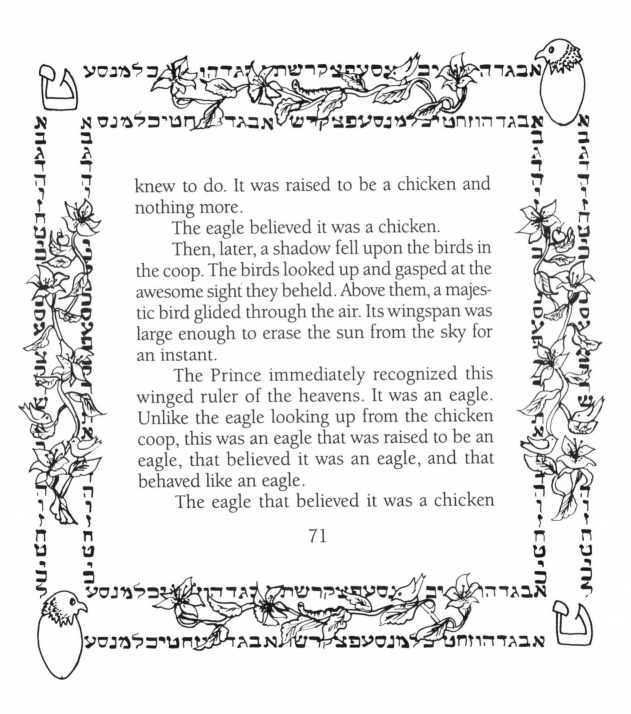

knew to do. It was raised to be a chicken and nothing more.

The eagle believed it was a chicken.

Then, later, a shadow fell upon the birds in the coop. The birds looked up and gasped at the awesome sight they beheld. Above them, a majestic bird glided through the air. Its wingspan was large enough to erase the sun from the sky for an instant.

The Prince immediately recognized this winged ruler of the heavens. It was an eagle. Unlike the eagle looking up from the chicken coop, this was an eagle that was raised to be an eagle, that believed it was an eagle, and that behaved like an eagle.

The eagle that believed it was a chicken

71

would never fly like that, would never soar upon the thrust of the wind or rise above the clouds. Just then the Prince understood how important it was for him to be true to himself and live like a prince.

72

A Dream Uninterpreted
Is Like a Treasure Unopened

When the Prince awakened, he blinked several times. Where was the Garden? Where was the mountain? Where was the chicken coop? Where were the eagles? His dream had been so vivid, he did not realize he had left that world and returned to the Waking World. He awakened in his bed, in his room, in the Palace.

Vivid dreams have such power that we continue to live in their world even after we awaken. Even the warm waters of the Prince's morning bath could not wash the dream from his life. The

75

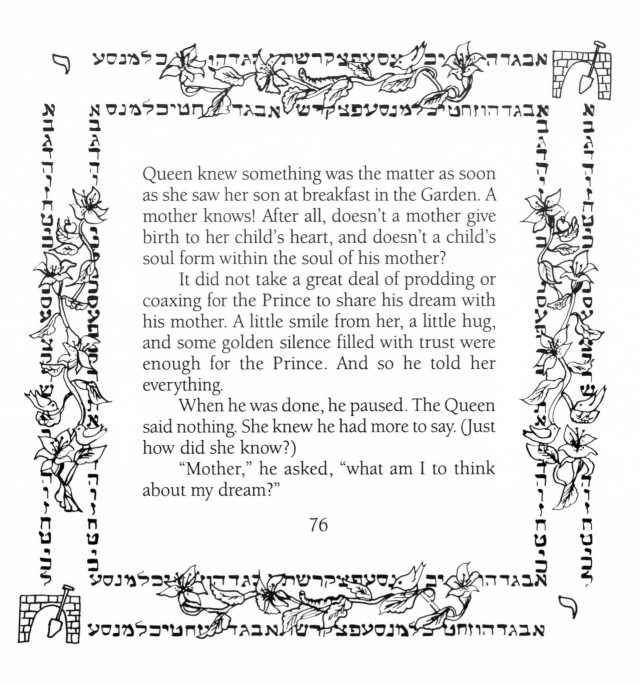

Queen knew something was the matter as soon as she saw her son at breakfast in the Garden. A mother knows! After all, doesn't a mother give birth to her child's heart, and doesn't a child's soul form within the soul of his mother?

It did not take a great deal of prodding or coaxing for the Prince to share his dream with his mother. A little smile from her, a little hug, and some golden silence filled with trust were enough for the Prince. And so he told her everything.

When he was done, he paused. The Queen said nothing. She knew he had more to say. (Just how did she know?)

"Mother," he asked, "what am I to think about my dream?"

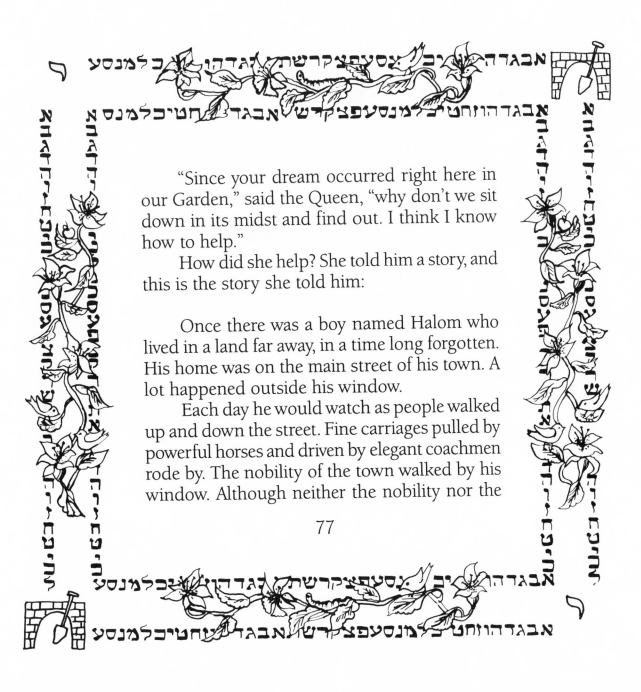

"Since your dream occurred right here in our Garden," said the Queen, "why don't we sit down in its midst and find out. I think I know how to help."

How did she help? She told him a story, and this is the story she told him:

Once there was a boy named Halom who lived in a land far away, in a time long forgotten. His home was on the main street of his town. A lot happened outside his window.

Each day he would watch as people walked up and down the street. Fine carriages pulled by powerful horses and driven by elegant coachmen rode by. The nobility of the town walked by his window. Although neither the nobility nor the

77

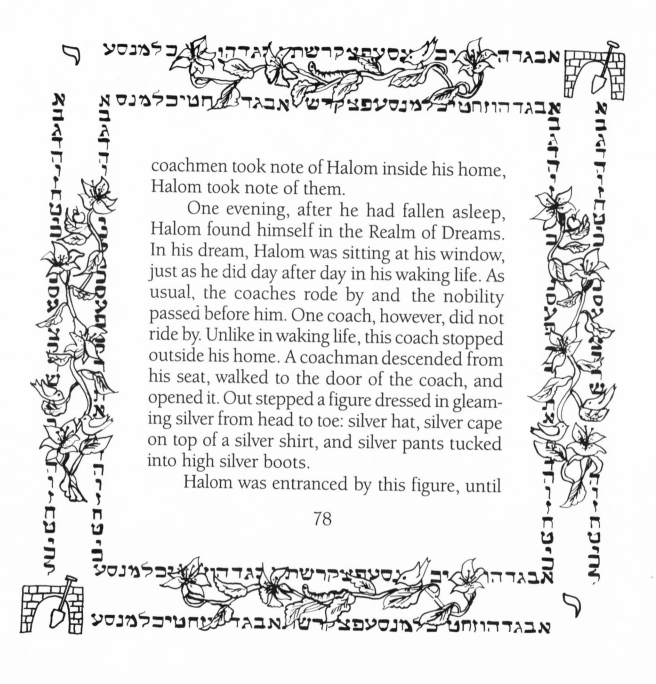

coachmen took note of Halom inside his home, Halom took note of them.

One evening, after he had fallen asleep, Halom found himself in the Realm of Dreams. In his dream, Halom was sitting at his window, just as he did day after day in his waking life. As usual, the coaches rode by and the nobility passed before him. One coach, however, did not ride by. Unlike in waking life, this coach stopped outside his home. A coachman descended from his seat, walked to the door of the coach, and opened it. Out stepped a figure dressed in gleaming silver from head to toe: silver hat, silver cape on top of a silver shirt, and silver pants tucked into high silver boots.

Halom was entranced by this figure, until

78

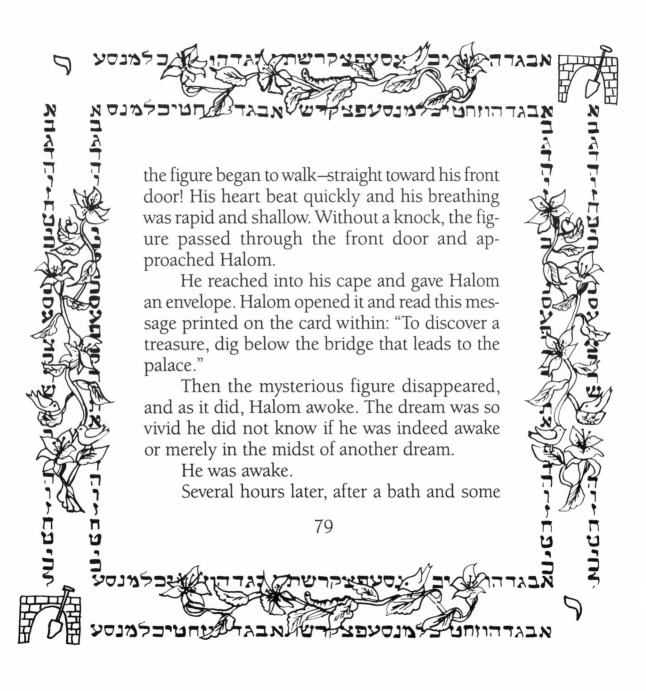

the figure began to walk—straight toward his front door! His heart beat quickly and his breathing was rapid and shallow. Without a knock, the figure passed through the front door and approached Halom.

He reached into his cape and gave Halom an envelope. Halom opened it and read this message printed on the card within: "To discover a treasure, dig below the bridge that leads to the palace."

Then the mysterious figure disappeared, and as it did, Halom awoke. The dream was so vivid he did not know if he was indeed awake or merely in the midst of another dream.

He was awake.

Several hours later, after a bath and some

79

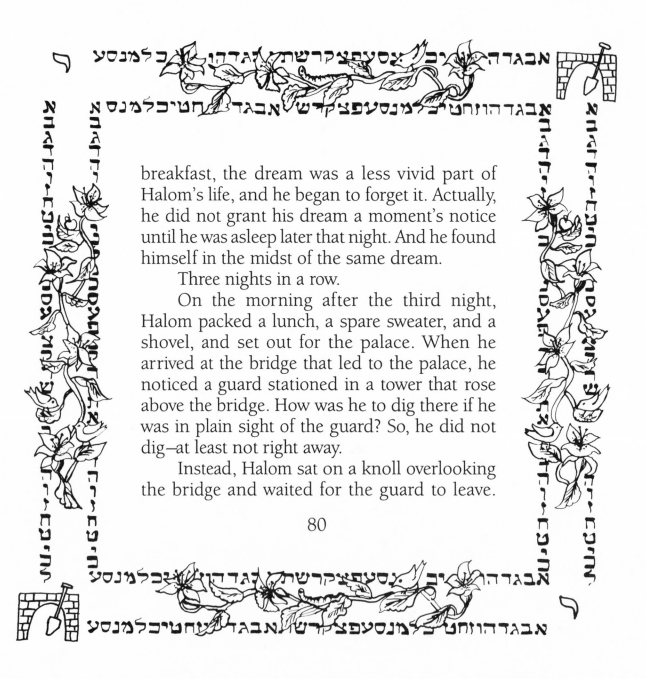

breakfast, the dream was a less vivid part of Halom's life, and he began to forget it. Actually, he did not grant his dream a moment's notice until he was asleep later that night. And he found himself in the midst of the same dream.

Three nights in a row.

On the morning after the third night, Halom packed a lunch, a spare sweater, and a shovel, and set out for the palace. When he arrived at the bridge that led to the palace, he noticed a guard stationed in a tower that rose above the bridge. How was he to dig there if he was in plain sight of the guard? So, he did not dig—at least not right away.

Instead, Halom sat on a knoll overlooking the bridge and waited for the guard to leave.

80

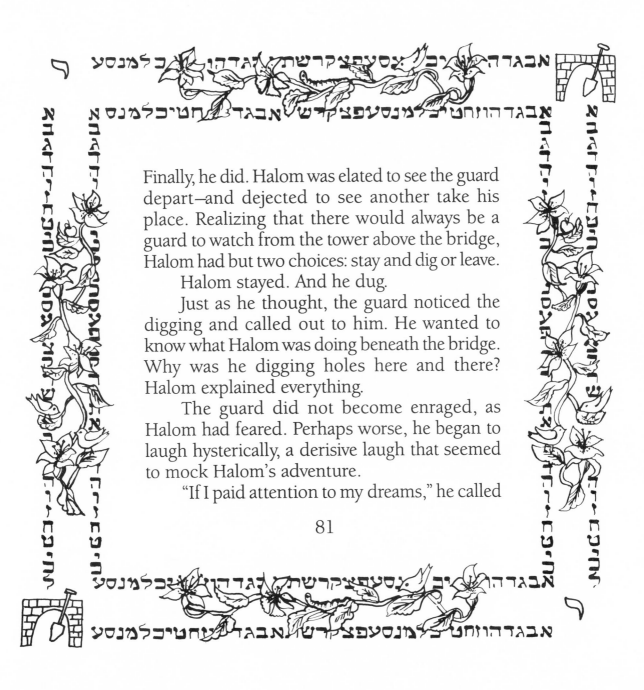

Finally, he did. Halom was elated to see the guard depart—and dejected to see another take his place. Realizing that there would always be a guard to watch from the tower above the bridge, Halom had but two choices: stay and dig or leave.

Halom stayed. And he dug.

Just as he thought, the guard noticed the digging and called out to him. He wanted to know what Halom was doing beneath the bridge. Why was he digging holes here and there? Halom explained everything.

The guard did not become enraged, as Halom had feared. Perhaps worse, he began to laugh hysterically, a derisive laugh that seemed to mock Halom's adventure.

"If I paid attention to my dreams," he called

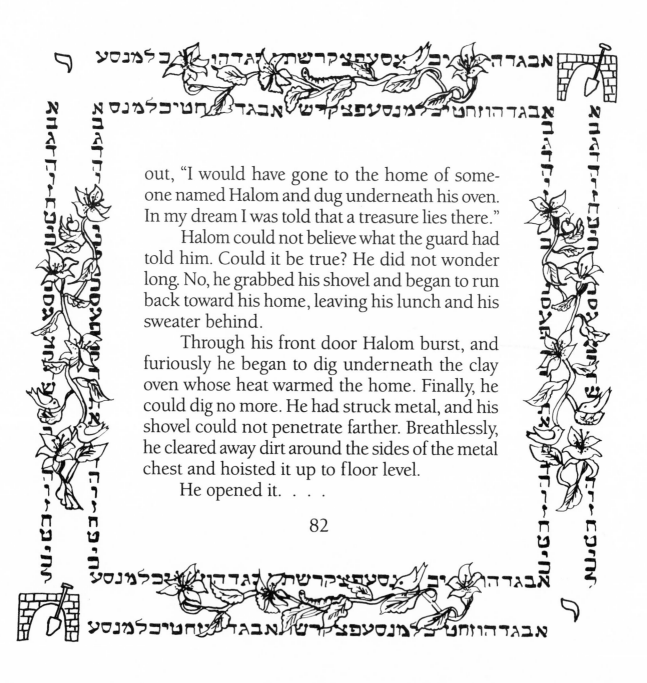

out, "I would have gone to the home of someone named Halom and dug underneath his oven.
In my dream I was told that a treasure lies there."

Halom could not believe what the guard had
told him. Could it be true? He did not wonder
long. No, he grabbed his shovel and began to run
back toward his home, leaving his lunch and his
sweater behind.

Through his front door Halom burst, and
furiously he began to dig underneath the clay
oven whose heat warmed the home. Finally, he
could dig no more. He had struck metal, and his
shovel could not penetrate farther. Breathlessly,
he cleared away dirt around the sides of the metal
chest and hoisted it up to floor level.

He opened it. . . .

82

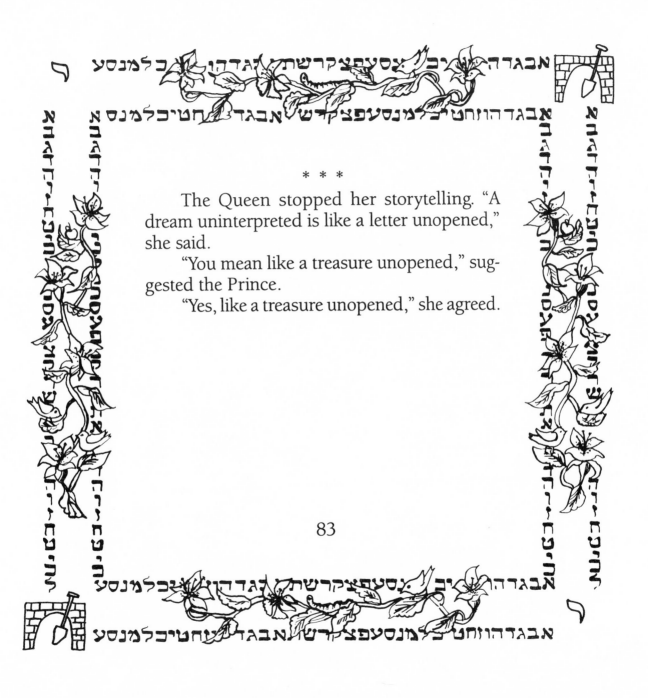

* * *

The Queen stopped her storytelling. "A dream uninterpreted is like a letter unopened," she said.

"You mean like a treasure unopened," suggested the Prince.

"Yes, like a treasure unopened," she agreed.

In Search of a Teacher

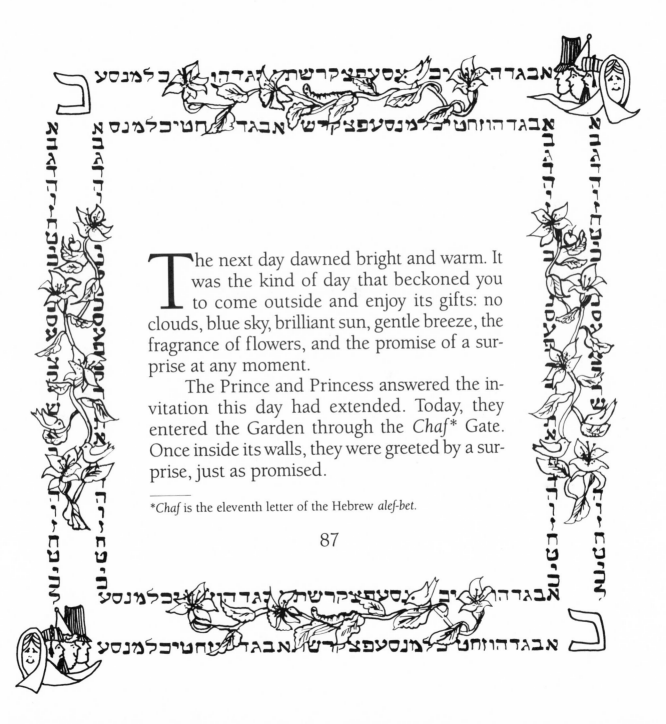

The next day dawned bright and warm. It was the kind of day that beckoned you to come outside and enjoy its gifts: no clouds, blue sky, brilliant sun, gentle breeze, the fragrance of flowers, and the promise of a surprise at any moment.

The Prince and Princess answered the invitation this day had extended. Today, they entered the Garden through the *Chaf** Gate. Once inside its walls, they were greeted by a surprise, just as promised.

---

*Chaf is the eleventh letter of the Hebrew *alef-bet*.

87

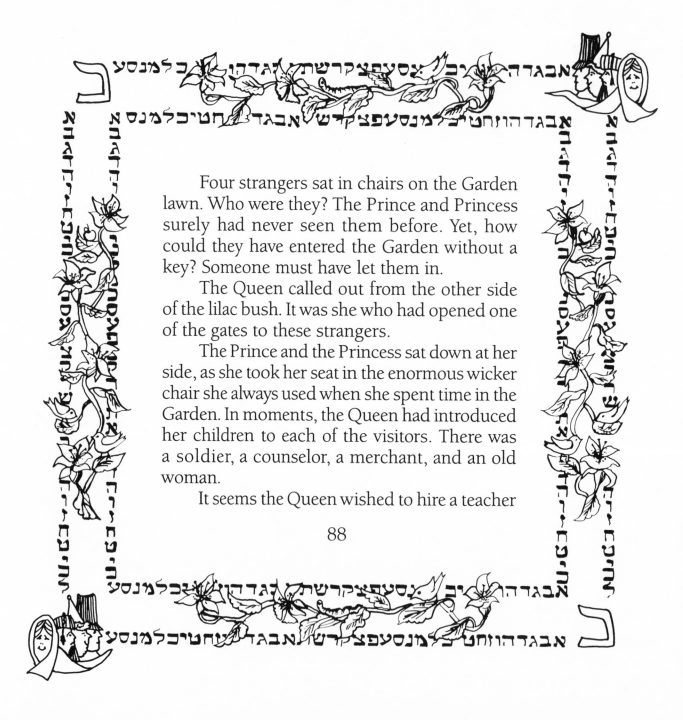

Four strangers sat in chairs on the Garden lawn. Who were they? The Prince and Princess surely had never seen them before. Yet, how could they have entered the Garden without a key? Someone must have let them in.

The Queen called out from the other side of the lilac bush. It was she who had opened one of the gates to these strangers.

The Prince and the Princess sat down at her side, as she took her seat in the enormous wicker chair she always used when she spent time in the Garden. In moments, the Queen had introduced her children to each of the visitors. There was a soldier, a counselor, a merchant, and an old woman.

It seems the Queen wished to hire a teacher

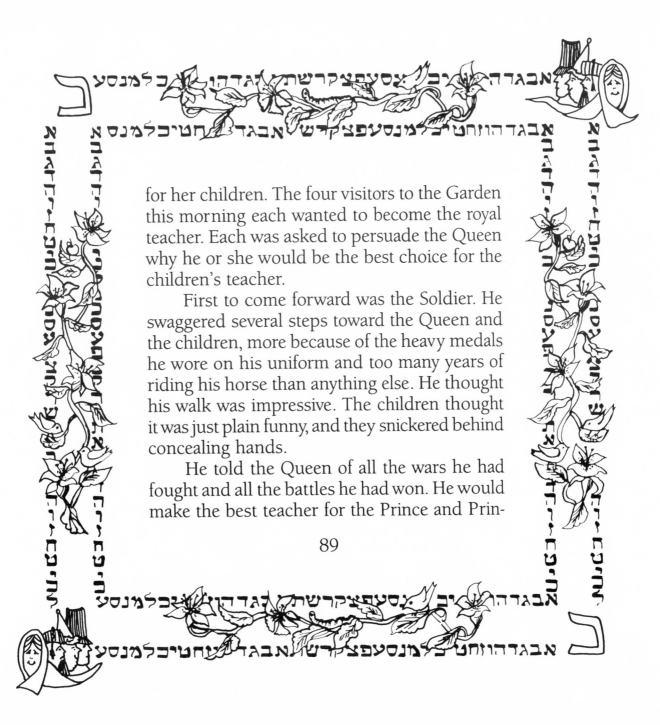

for her children. The four visitors to the Garden this morning each wanted to become the royal teacher. Each was asked to persuade the Queen why he or she would be the best choice for the children's teacher.

First to come forward was the Soldier. He swaggered several steps toward the Queen and the children, more because of the heavy medals he wore on his uniform and too many years of riding his horse than anything else. He thought his walk was impressive. The children thought it was just plain funny, and they snickered behind concealing hands.

He told the Queen of all the wars he had fought and all the battles he had won. He would make the best teacher for the Prince and Prin-

89

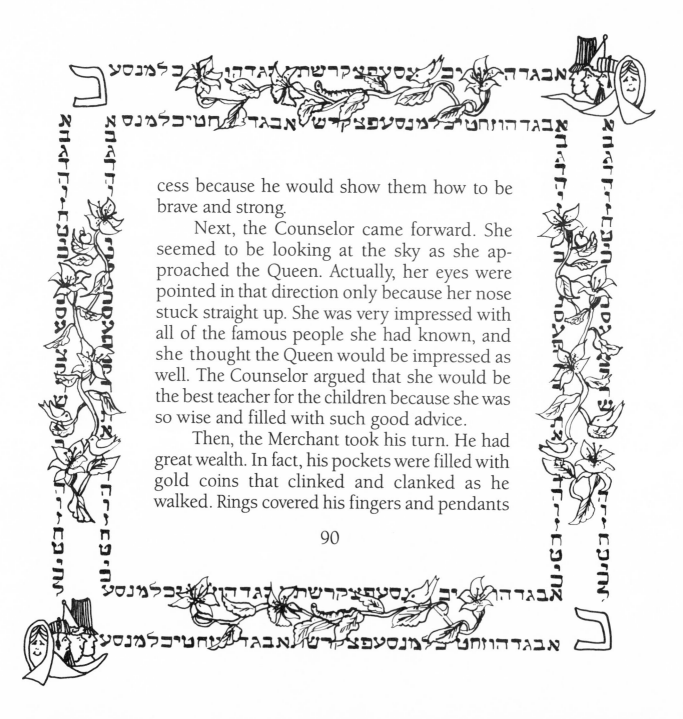

cess because he would show them how to be brave and strong.

Next, the Counselor came forward. She seemed to be looking at the sky as she approached the Queen. Actually, her eyes were pointed in that direction only because her nose stuck straight up. She was very impressed with all of the famous people she had known, and she thought the Queen would be impressed as well. The Counselor argued that she would be the best teacher for the children because she was so wise and filled with such good advice.

Then, the Merchant took his turn. He had great wealth. In fact, his pockets were filled with gold coins that clinked and clanked as he walked. Rings covered his fingers and pendants

90

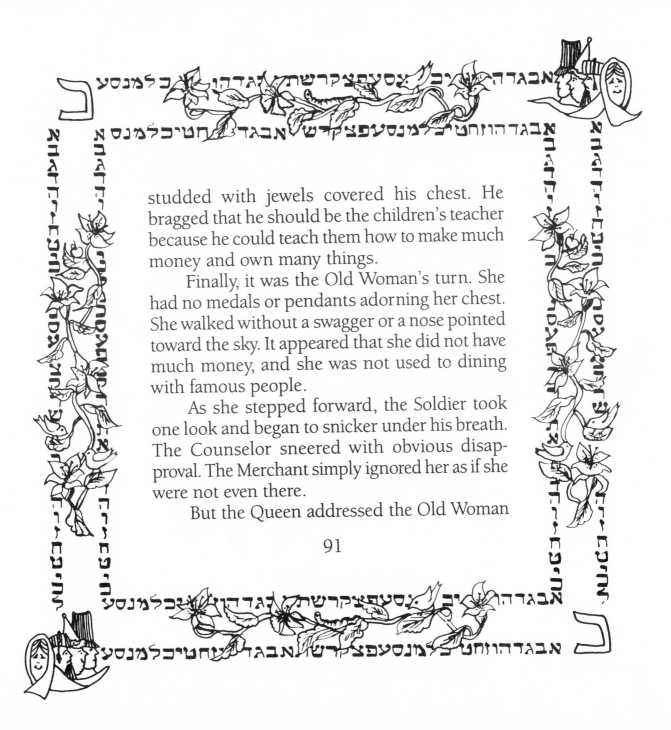

studded with jewels covered his chest. He bragged that he should be the children's teacher because he could teach them how to make much money and own many things.

Finally, it was the Old Woman's turn. She had no medals or pendants adorning her chest. She walked without a swagger or a nose pointed toward the sky. It appeared that she did not have much money, and she was not used to dining with famous people.

As she stepped forward, the Soldier took one look and began to snicker under his breath. The Counselor sneered with obvious disapproval. The Merchant simply ignored her as if she were not even there.

But the Queen addressed the Old Woman

91

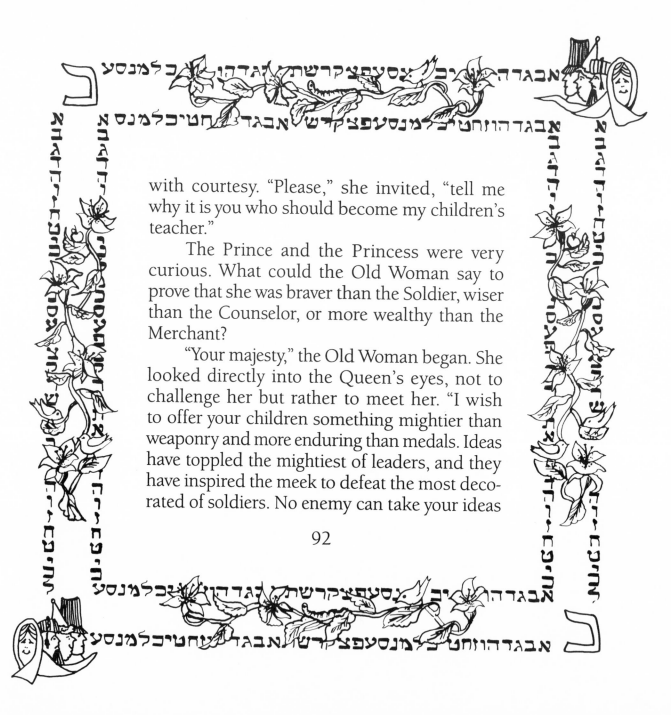

with courtesy. "Please," she invited, "tell me why it is you who should become my children's teacher."

The Prince and the Princess were very curious. What could the Old Woman say to prove that she was braver than the Soldier, wiser than the Counselor, or more wealthy than the Merchant?

"Your majesty," the Old Woman began. She looked directly into the Queen's eyes, not to challenge her but rather to meet her. "I wish to offer your children something mightier than weaponry and more enduring than medals. Ideas have toppled the mightiest of leaders, and they have inspired the meek to defeat the most decorated of soldiers. No enemy can take your ideas

92

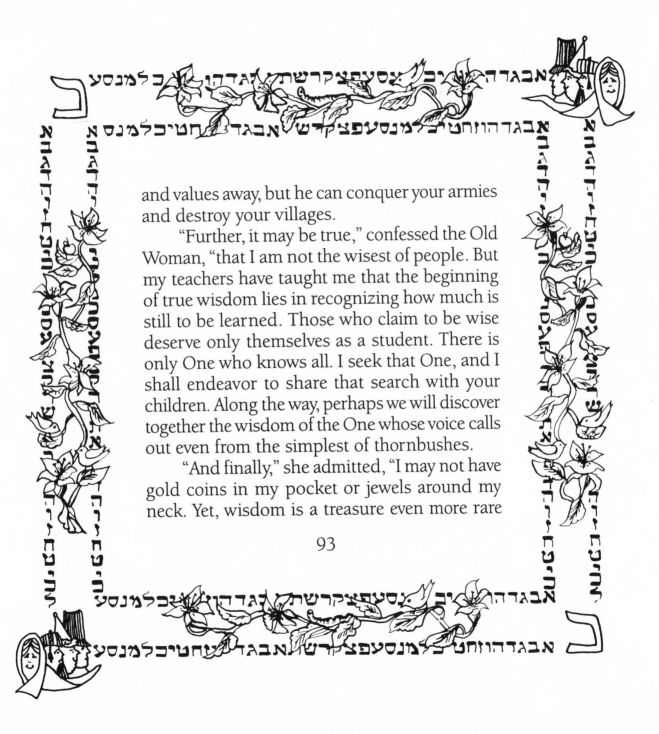

and values away, but he can conquer your armies and destroy your villages.

"Further, it may be true," confessed the Old Woman, "that I am not the wisest of people. But my teachers have taught me that the beginning of true wisdom lies in recognizing how much is still to be learned. Those who claim to be wise deserve only themselves as a student. There is only One who knows all. I seek that One, and I shall endeavor to share that search with your children. Along the way, perhaps we will discover together the wisdom of the One whose voice calls out even from the simplest of thornbushes.

"And finally," she admitted, "I may not have gold coins in my pocket or jewels around my neck. Yet, wisdom is a treasure even more rare

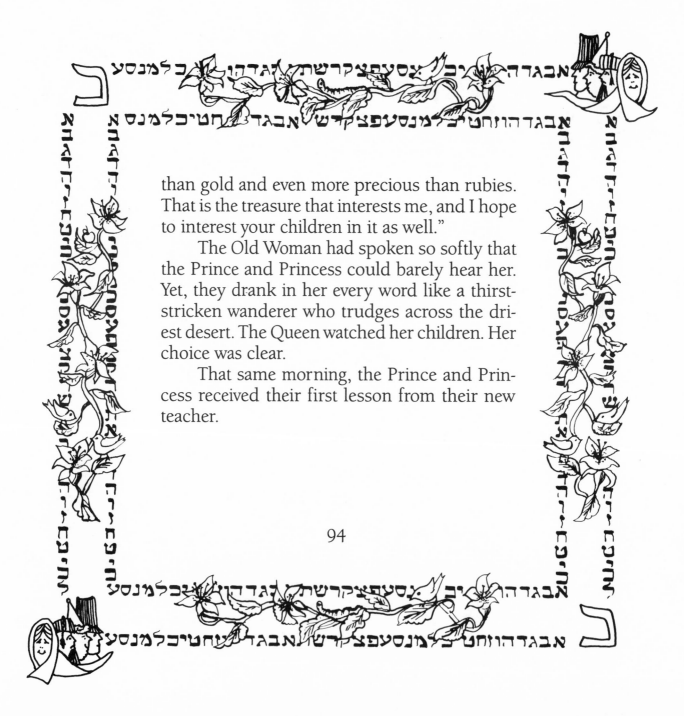

than gold and even more precious than rubies. That is the treasure that interests me, and I hope to interest your children in it as well."

The Old Woman had spoken so softly that the Prince and Princess could barely hear her. Yet, they drank in her every word like a thirst-stricken wanderer who trudges across the driest desert. The Queen watched her children. Her choice was clear.

That same morning, the Prince and Princess received their first lesson from their new teacher.

One

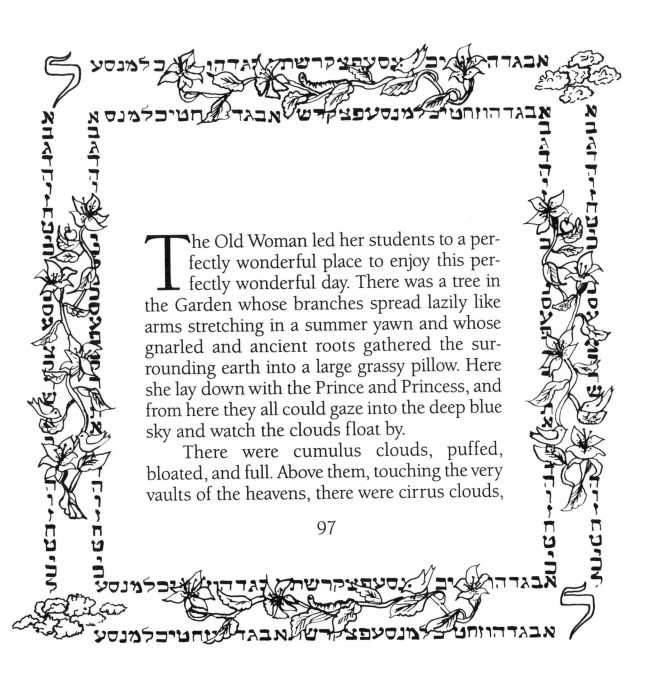

The Old Woman led her students to a perfectly wonderful place to enjoy this perfectly wonderful day. There was a tree in the Garden whose branches spread lazily like arms stretching in a summer yawn and whose gnarled and ancient roots gathered the surrounding earth into a large grassy pillow. Here she lay down with the Prince and Princess, and from here they all could gaze into the deep blue sky and watch the clouds float by.

There were cumulus clouds, puffed, bloated, and full. Above them, touching the very vaults of the heavens, there were cirrus clouds,

97

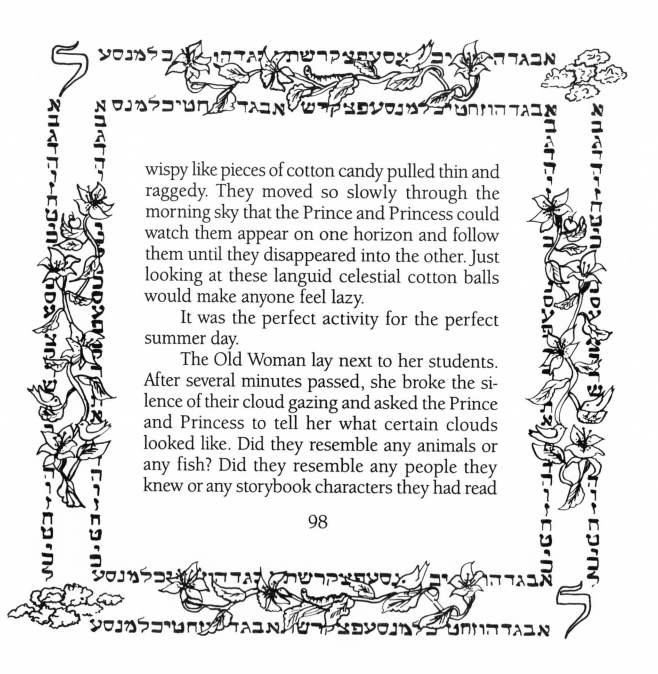

wispy like pieces of cotton candy pulled thin and raggedy. They moved so slowly through the morning sky that the Prince and Princess could watch them appear on one horizon and follow them until they disappeared into the other. Just looking at these languid celestial cotton balls would make anyone feel lazy.

It was the perfect activity for the perfect summer day.

The Old Woman lay next to her students. After several minutes passed, she broke the silence of their cloud gazing and asked the Prince and Princess to tell her what certain clouds looked like. Did they resemble any animals or any fish? Did they resemble any people they knew or any storybook characters they had read

98

about? Did they resemble objects like houses or boats? Did they resemble plants or trees? The Old Woman was curious. "What do they look like?" she asked.

The Prince responded right away. Usually, one child in a family is first to respond. The Prince was always the first to respond in this family. And the Princess let him do so.

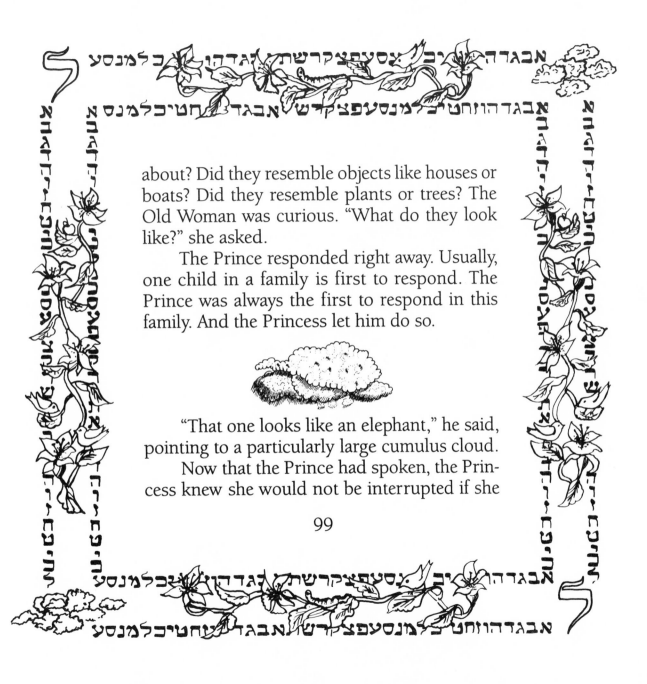

"That one looks like an elephant," he said, pointing to a particularly large cumulus cloud.

Now that the Prince had spoken, the Princess knew she would not be interrupted if she spoke. She looked around for a moment, and then she spotted her cloud. "I think that one over there looks like a flying bird," she said.

They took turns pointing out what this cloud looked like and what that one looked like for the longest time. Imagine what they saw in clouds like these:

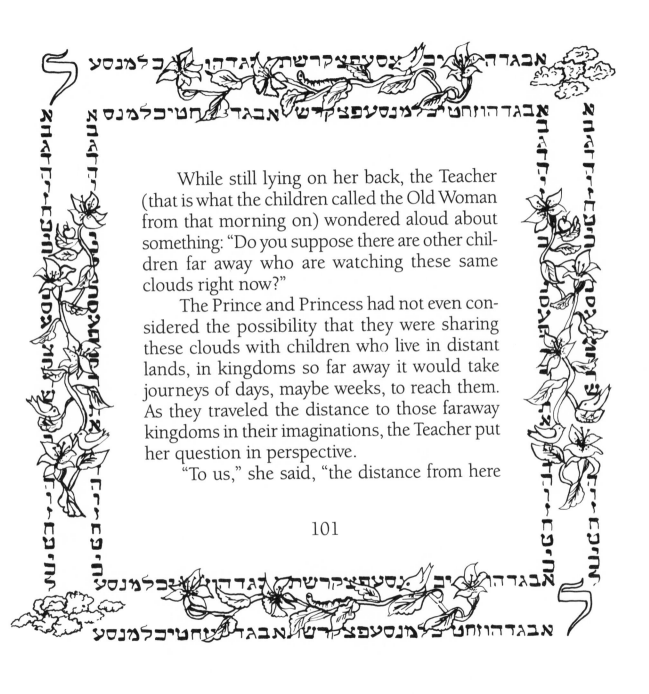

While still lying on her back, the Teacher (that is what the children called the Old Woman from that morning on) wondered aloud about something: "Do you suppose there are other children far away who are watching these same clouds right now?"

The Prince and Princess had not even considered the possibility that they were sharing these clouds with children who live in distant lands, in kingdoms so far away it would take journeys of days, maybe weeks, to reach them. As they traveled the distance to those faraway kingdoms in their imaginations, the Teacher put her question in perspective.

"To us," she said, "the distance from here

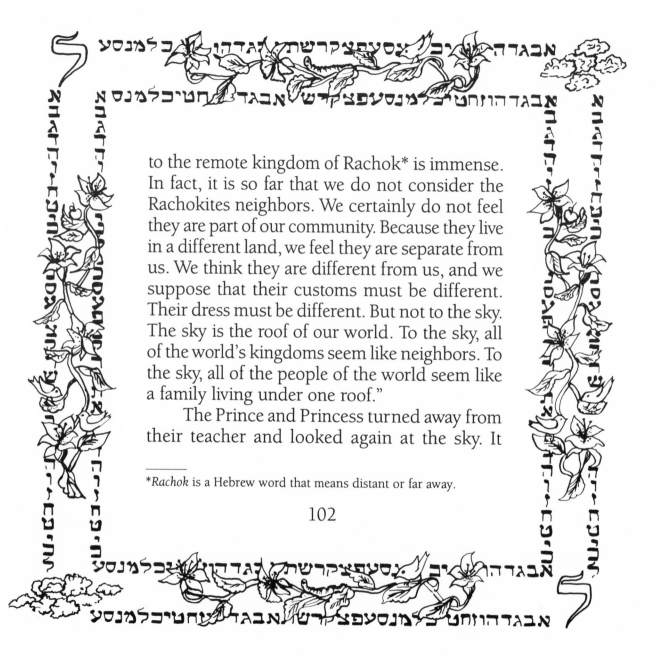

to the remote kingdom of Rachok* is immense. In fact, it is so far that we do not consider the Rachokites neighbors. We certainly do not feel they are part of our community. Because they live in a different land, we feel they are separate from us. We think they are different from us, and we suppose that their customs must be different. Their dress must be different. But not to the sky. The sky is the roof of our world. To the sky, all of the world's kingdoms seem like neighbors. To the sky, all of the people of the world seem like a family living under one roof."

The Prince and Princess turned away from their teacher and looked again at the sky. It

---

Rachok is a Hebrew word that means distant or far away.

102

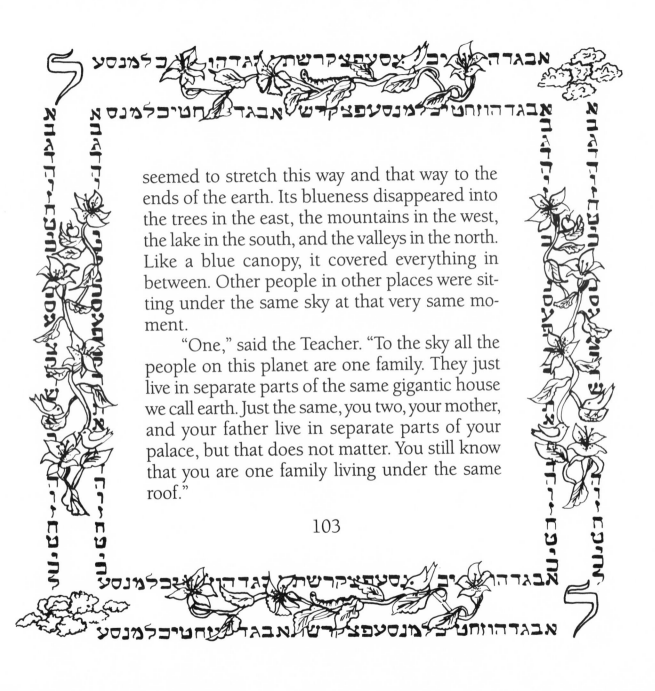

seemed to stretch this way and that way to the ends of the earth. Its blueness disappeared into the trees in the east, the mountains in the west, the lake in the south, and the valleys in the north. Like a blue canopy, it covered everything in between. Other people in other places were sitting under the same sky at that very same moment.

"One," said the Teacher. "To the sky all the people on this planet are one family. They just live in separate parts of the same gigantic house we call earth. Just the same, you two, your mother, and your father live in separate parts of your palace, but that does not matter. You still know that you are one family living under the same roof."

103

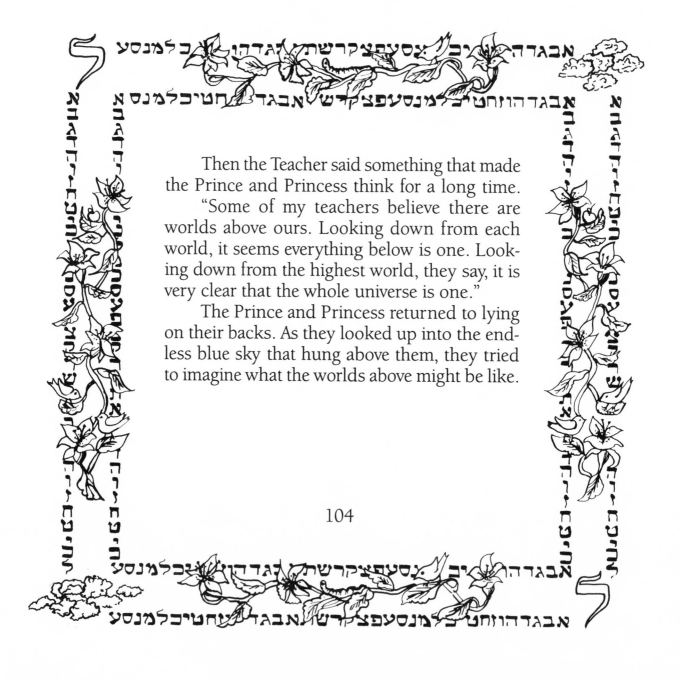

Then the Teacher said something that made the Prince and Princess think for a long time.

"Some of my teachers believe there are worlds above ours. Looking down from each world, it seems everything below is one. Looking down from the highest world, they say, it is very clear that the whole universe is one."

The Prince and Princess returned to lying on their backs. As they looked up into the endless blue sky that hung above them, they tried to imagine what the worlds above might be like.

The Opal

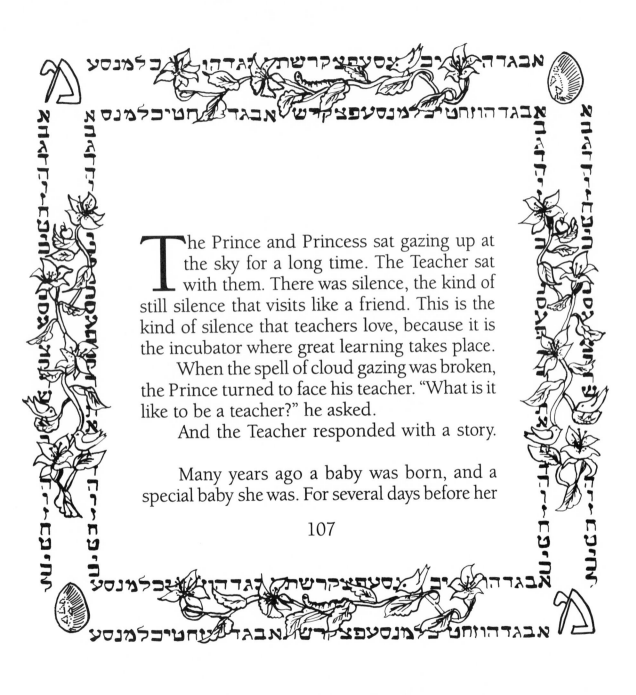

The Prince and Princess sat gazing up at the sky for a long time. The Teacher sat with them. There was silence, the kind of still silence that visits like a friend. This is the kind of silence that teachers love, because it is the incubator where great learning takes place.

When the spell of cloud gazing was broken, the Prince turned to face his teacher. "What is it like to be a teacher?" he asked.

And the Teacher responded with a story.

Many years ago a baby was born, and a special baby she was. For several days before her

107

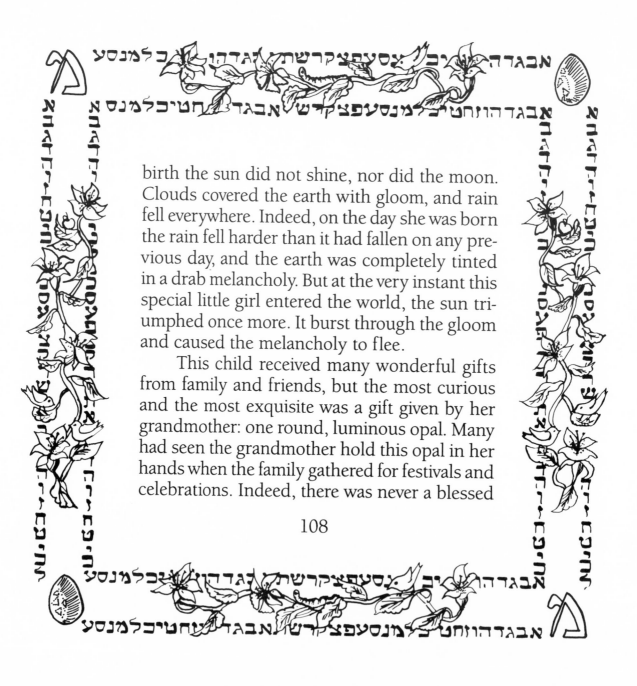

birth the sun did not shine, nor did the moon. Clouds covered the earth with gloom, and rain fell everywhere. Indeed, on the day she was born the rain fell harder than it had fallen on any previous day, and the earth was completely tinted in a drab melancholy. But at the very instant this special little girl entered the world, the sun triumphed once more. It burst through the gloom and caused the melancholy to flee.

This child received many wonderful gifts from family and friends, but the most curious and the most exquisite was a gift given by her grandmother: one round, luminous opal. Many had seen the grandmother hold this opal in her hands when the family gathered for festivals and celebrations. Indeed, there was never a blessed

108

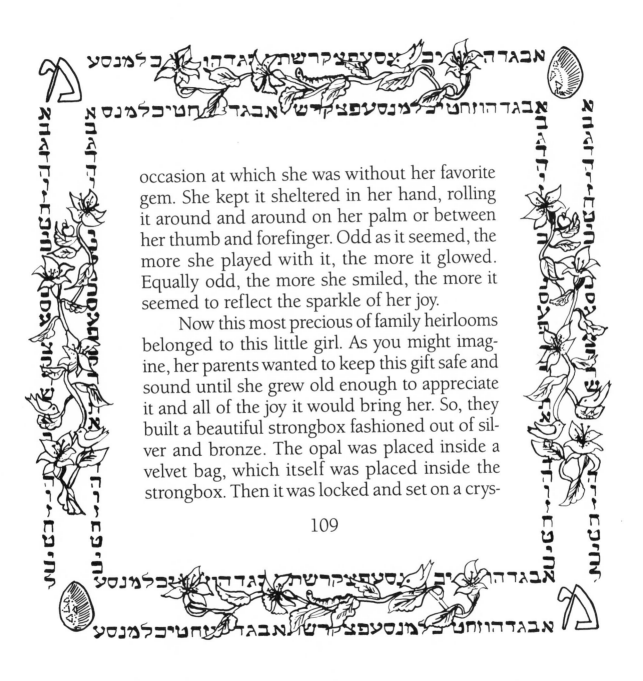

occasion at which she was without her favorite gem. She kept it sheltered in her hand, rolling it around and around on her palm or between her thumb and forefinger. Odd as it seemed, the more she played with it, the more it glowed. Equally odd, the more she smiled, the more it seemed to reflect the sparkle of her joy.

Now this most precious of family heirlooms belonged to this little girl. As you might imagine, her parents wanted to keep this gift safe and sound until she grew old enough to appreciate it and all of the joy it would bring her. So, they built a beautiful strongbox fashioned out of silver and bronze. The opal was placed inside a velvet bag, which itself was placed inside the strongbox. Then it was locked and set on a crys-

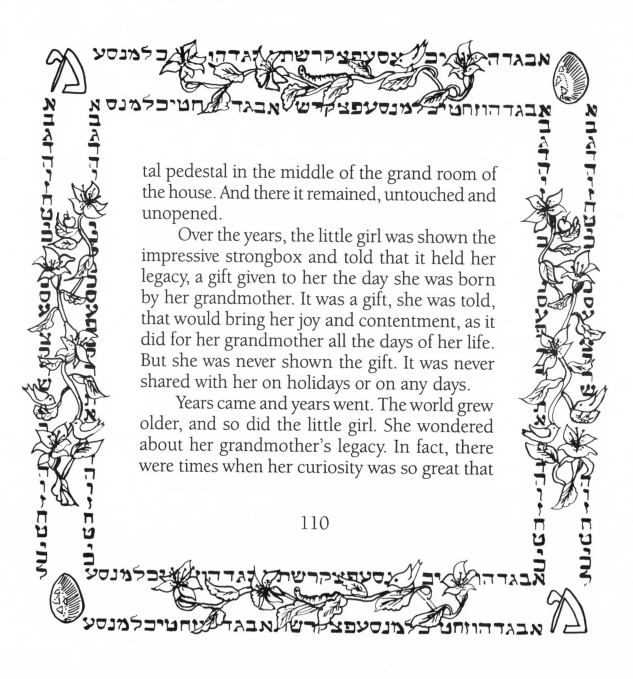

tal pedestal in the middle of the grand room of the house. And there it remained, untouched and unopened.

Over the years, the little girl was shown the impressive strongbox and told that it held her legacy, a gift given to her the day she was born by her grandmother. It was a gift, she was told, that would bring her joy and contentment, as it did for her grandmother all the days of her life. But she was never shown the gift. It was never shared with her on holidays or on any days.

Years came and years went. The world grew older, and so did the little girl. She wondered about her grandmother's legacy. In fact, there were times when her curiosity was so great that

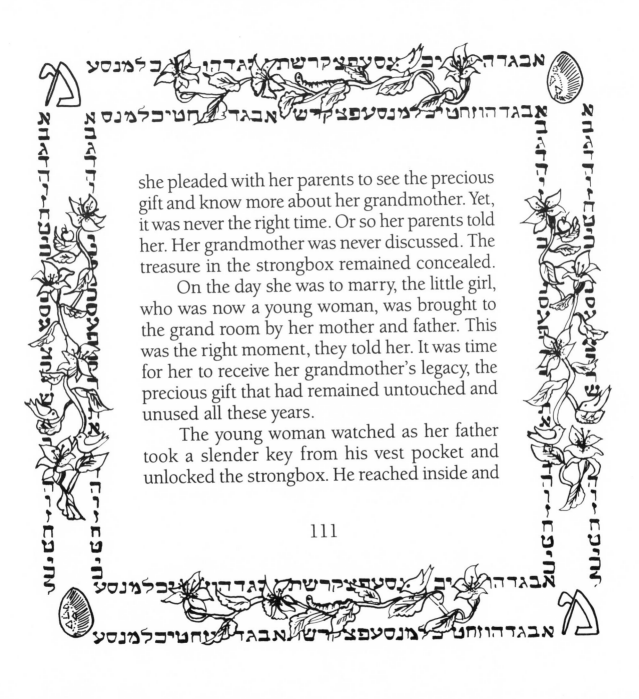

she pleaded with her parents to see the precious gift and know more about her grandmother. Yet, it was never the right time. Or so her parents told her. Her grandmother was never discussed. The treasure in the strongbox remained concealed.

On the day she was to marry, the little girl, who was now a young woman, was brought to the grand room by her mother and father. This was the right moment, they told her. It was time for her to receive her grandmother's legacy, the precious gift that had remained untouched and unused all these years.

The young woman watched as her father took a slender key from his vest pocket and unlocked the strongbox. He reached inside and

111

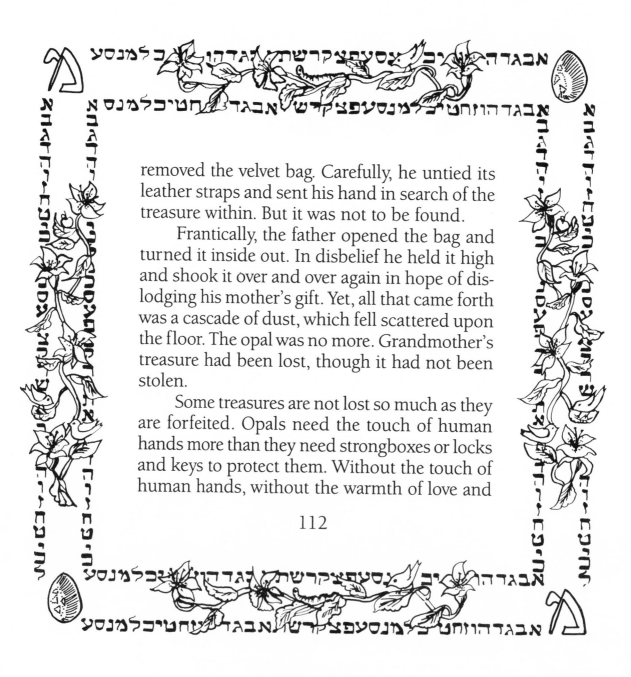

removed the velvet bag. Carefully, he untied its leather straps and sent his hand in search of the treasure within. But it was not to be found.

Frantically, the father opened the bag and turned it inside out. In disbelief he held it high and shook it over and over again in hope of dislodging his mother's gift. Yet, all that came forth was a cascade of dust, which fell scattered upon the floor. The opal was no more. Grandmother's treasure had been lost, though it had not been stolen.

Some treasures are not lost so much as they are forfeited. Opals need the touch of human hands more than they need strongboxes or locks and keys to protect them. Without the touch of human hands, without the warmth of love and

112

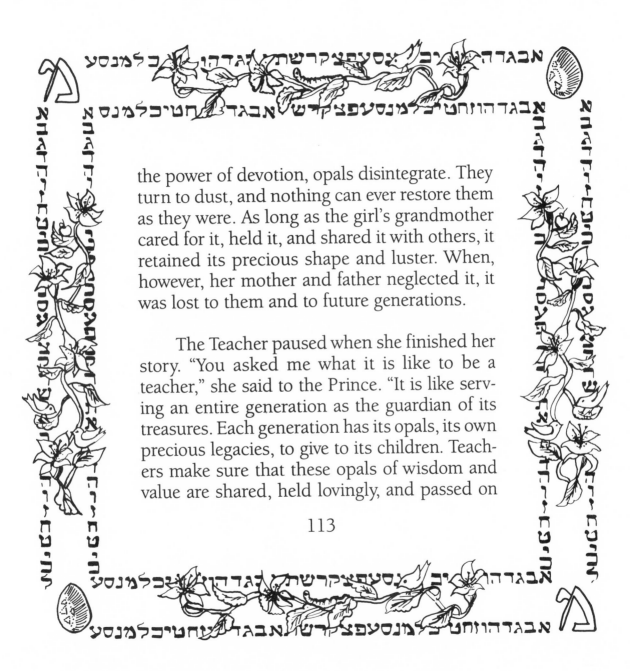

the power of devotion, opals disintegrate. They turn to dust, and nothing can ever restore them as they were. As long as the girl's grandmother cared for it, held it, and shared it with others, it retained its precious shape and luster. When, however, her mother and father neglected it, it was lost to them and to future generations.

The Teacher paused when she finished her story. "You asked me what it is like to be a teacher," she said to the Prince. "It is like serving an entire generation as the guardian of its treasures. Each generation has its opals, its own precious legacies, to give to its children. Teachers make sure that these opals of wisdom and value are shared, held lovingly, and passed on

113

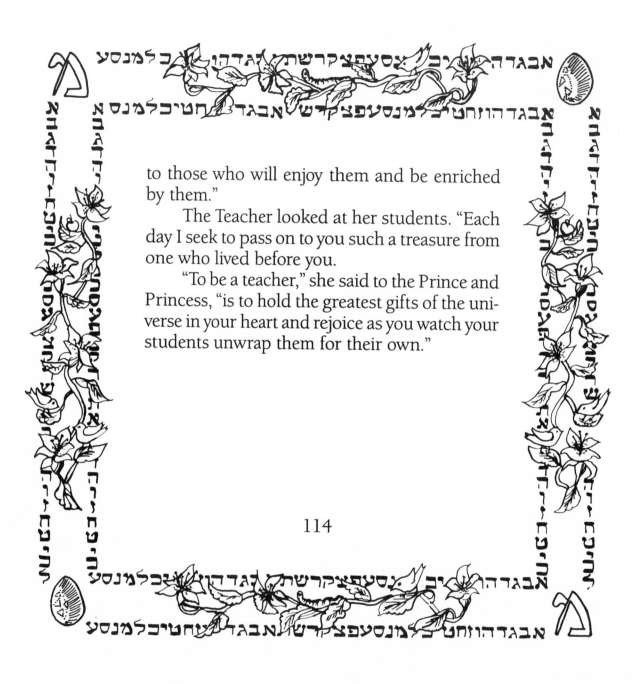

to those who will enjoy them and be enriched by them."

The Teacher looked at her students. "Each day I seek to pass on to you such a treasure from one who lived before you.

"To be a teacher," she said to the Prince and Princess, "is to hold the greatest gifts of the universe in your heart and rejoice as you watch your students unwrap them for their own."

114

The Inheritance

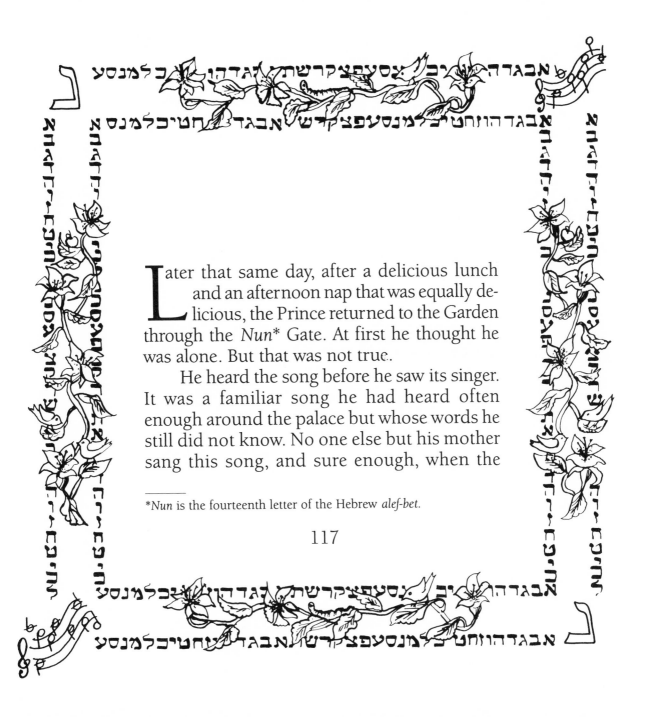

Later that same day, after a delicious lunch and an afternoon nap that was equally delicious, the Prince returned to the Garden through the *Nun** Gate. At first he thought he was alone. But that was not true.

He heard the song before he saw its singer. It was a familiar song he had heard often enough around the palace but whose words he still did not know. No one else but his mother sang this song, and sure enough, when the

---

Nun is the fourteenth letter of the Hebrew *alef-bet*.

117

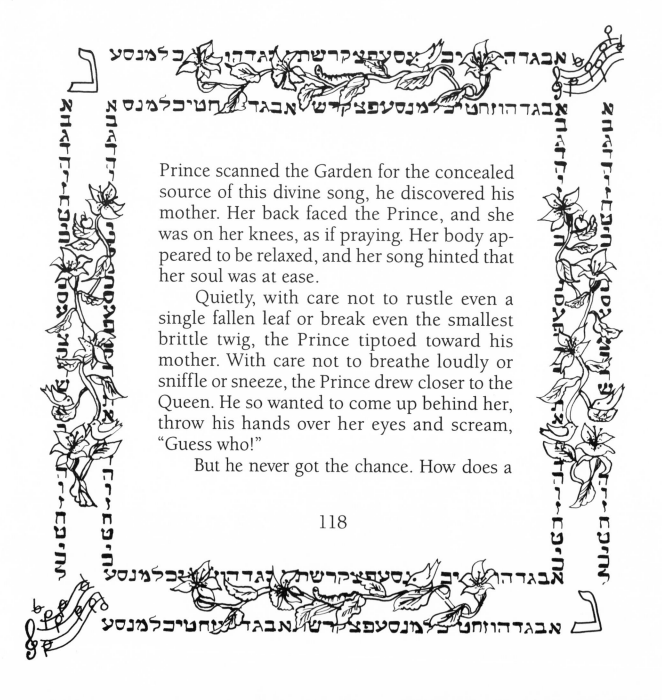

Prince scanned the Garden for the concealed source of this divine song, he discovered his mother. Her back faced the Prince, and she was on her knees, as if praying. Her body appeared to be relaxed, and her song hinted that her soul was at ease.

Quietly, with care not to rustle even a single fallen leaf or break even the smallest brittle twig, the Prince tiptoed toward his mother. With care not to breathe loudly or sniffle or sneeze, the Prince drew closer to the Queen. He so wanted to come up behind her, throw his hands over her eyes and scream, "Guess who!"

But he never got the chance. How does a

118

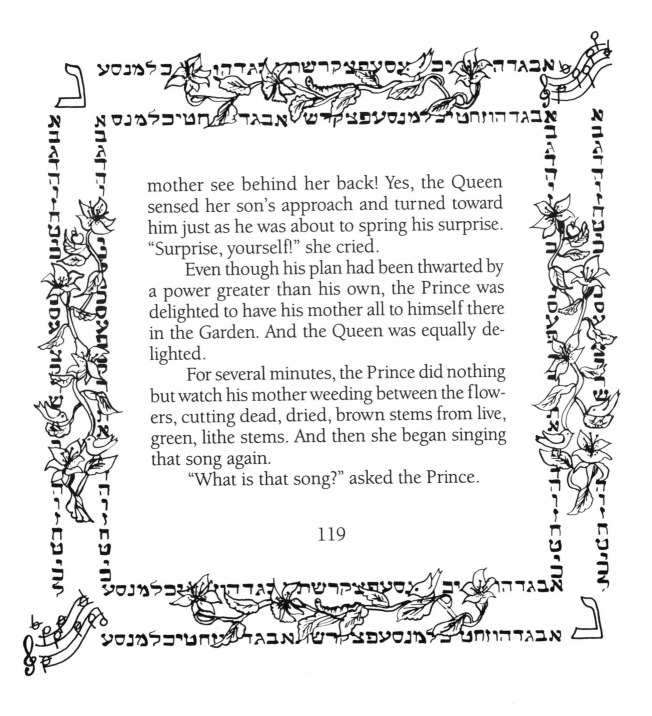

mother see behind her back! Yes, the Queen sensed her son's approach and turned toward him just as he was about to spring his surprise. "Surprise, yourself!" she cried.

Even though his plan had been thwarted by a power greater than his own, the Prince was delighted to have his mother all to himself there in the Garden. And the Queen was equally delighted.

For several minutes, the Prince did nothing but watch his mother weeding between the flowers, cutting dead, dried, brown stems from live, green, lithe stems. And then she began singing that song again.

"What is that song?" asked the Prince.

119

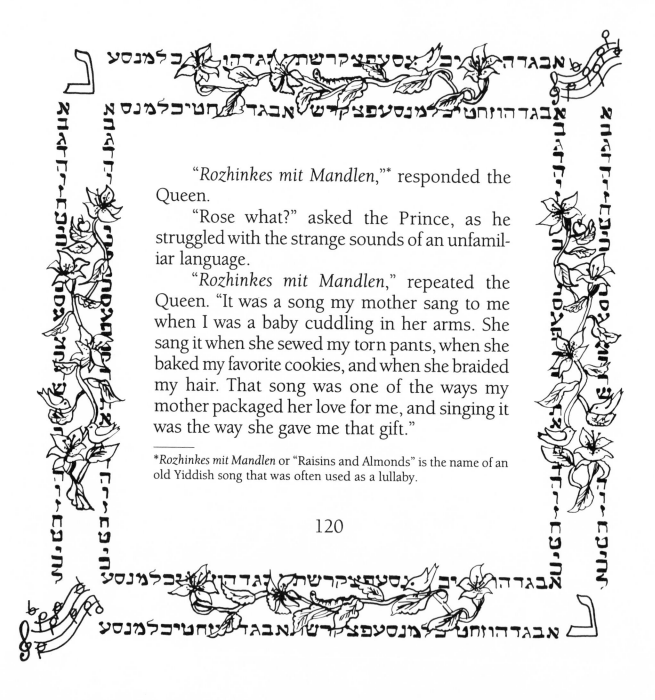

"*Rozhinkes mit Mandlen*,"* responded the Queen.

"Rose what?" asked the Prince, as he struggled with the strange sounds of an unfamiliar language.

"*Rozhinkes mit Mandlen*," repeated the Queen. "It was a song my mother sang to me when I was a baby cuddling in her arms. She sang it when she sewed my torn pants, when she baked my favorite cookies, and when she braided my hair. That song was one of the ways my mother packaged her love for me, and singing it was the way she gave me that gift."

Rozhinkes mit Mandlen or "Raisins and Almonds" is the name of an old Yiddish song that was often used as a lullaby.

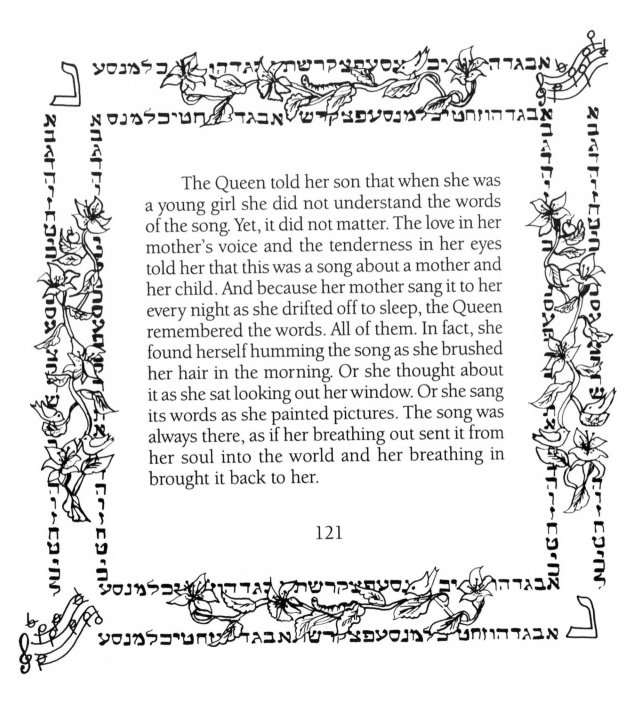

The Queen told her son that when she was a young girl she did not understand the words of the song. Yet, it did not matter. The love in her mother's voice and the tenderness in her eyes told her that this was a song about a mother and her child. And because her mother sang it to her every night as she drifted off to sleep, the Queen remembered the words. All of them. In fact, she found herself humming the song as she brushed her hair in the morning. Or she thought about it as she sat looking out her window. Or she sang its words as she painted pictures. The song was always there, as if her breathing out sent it from her soul into the world and her breathing in brought it back to her.

121

"My mother told me that song was my *yerushah*,"* said the Queen, turning to the Prince. She had stopped remembering her childhood now and had returned to the beautiful afternoon she was spending with her son.

"*Yerushah*?" asked the Prince. It was clear that he did not understand.

"Yes, my darling son," said the Queen. "She meant my inheritance. It is one of the ways she is always with me. My smile is from her. The color of my eyes and hair are from her. My laugh is from her. Even the way I sneeze is from her. That song is from her, too. Sometimes when I look in the mirror, I glimpse some of my mother.

---

*Yerushah is a Hebrew word meaning "inheritance" or "legacy."

And sometimes when I sing that song, I feel my mother here with me."

The Queen reached forward to stroke her son's cheek.

"A song is a *yerushah*. This song is your *yerushah*, if you want it."

If the song would help the Prince keep his mother with him forever, then he wanted it.

"Yes," he said. "I want it."

So, the Queen taught the Prince that song.

The King Who Thought
He Was a Turkey

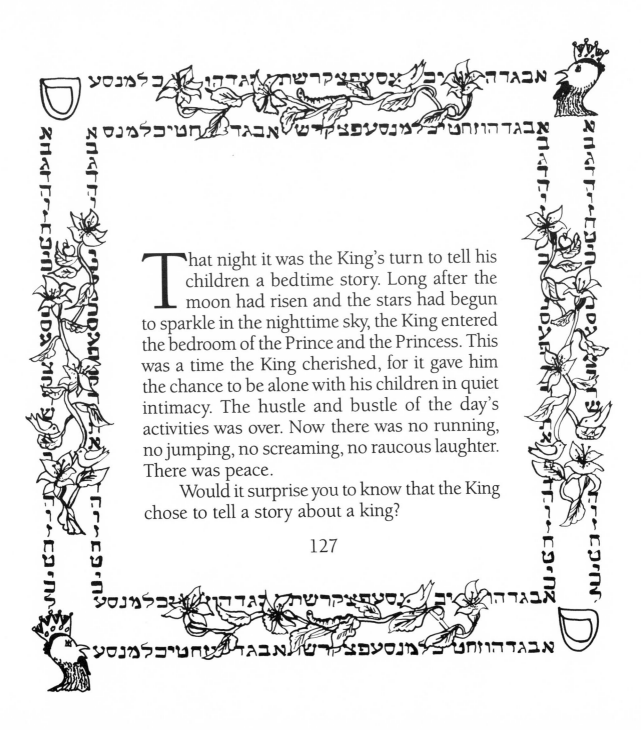

That night it was the King's turn to tell his children a bedtime story. Long after the moon had risen and the stars had begun to sparkle in the nighttime sky, the King entered the bedroom of the Prince and the Princess. This was a time the King cherished, for it gave him the chance to be alone with his children in quiet intimacy. The hustle and bustle of the day's activities was over. Now there was no running, no jumping, no screaming, no raucous laughter. There was peace.

Would it surprise you to know that the King chose to tell a story about a king?

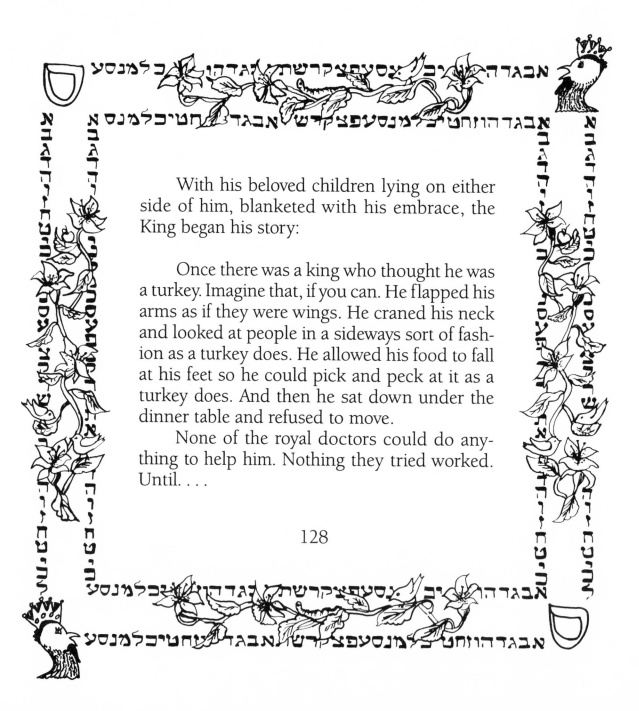

With his beloved children lying on either side of him, blanketed with his embrace, the King began his story:

Once there was a king who thought he was a turkey. Imagine that, if you can. He flapped his arms as if they were wings. He craned his neck and looked at people in a sideways sort of fashion as a turkey does. He allowed his food to fall at his feet so he could pick and peck at it as a turkey does. And then he sat down under the dinner table and refused to move.

None of the royal doctors could do anything to help him. Nothing they tried worked. Until. . . .

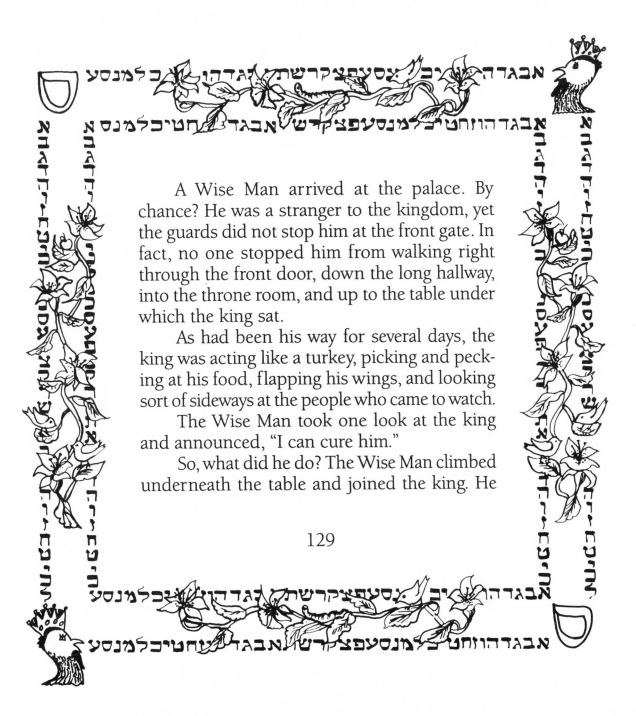

A Wise Man arrived at the palace. By chance? He was a stranger to the kingdom, yet the guards did not stop him at the front gate. In fact, no one stopped him from walking right through the front door, down the long hallway, into the throne room, and up to the table under which the king sat.

As had been his way for several days, the king was acting like a turkey, picking and pecking at his food, flapping his wings, and looking sort of sideways at the people who came to watch.

The Wise Man took one look at the king and announced, "I can cure him."

So, what did he do? The Wise Man climbed underneath the table and joined the king. He

129

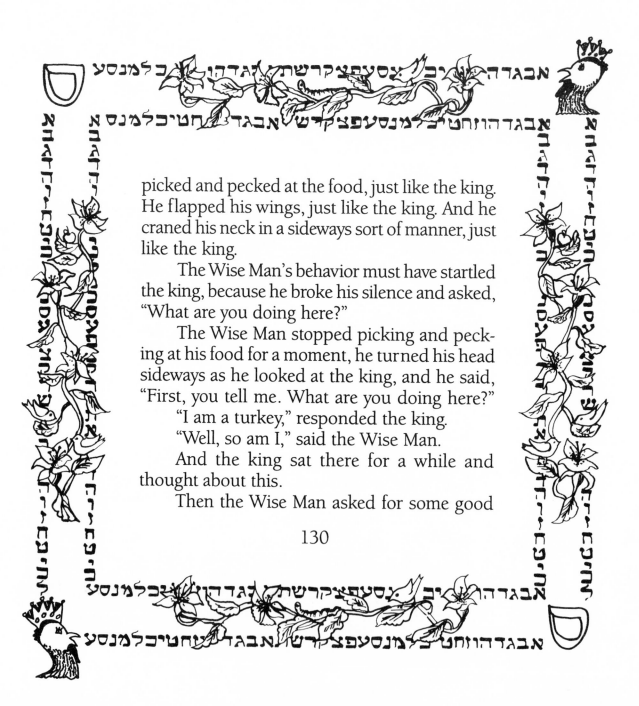

picked and pecked at the food, just like the king. He flapped his wings, just like the king. And he craned his neck in a sideways sort of manner, just like the king.

The Wise Man's behavior must have startled the king, because he broke his silence and asked, "What are you doing here?"

The Wise Man stopped picking and pecking at his food for a moment, he turned his head sideways as he looked at the king, and he said, "First, you tell me. What are you doing here?"

"I am a turkey," responded the king.

"Well, so am I," said the Wise Man.

And the king sat there for a while and thought about this.

Then the Wise Man asked for some good

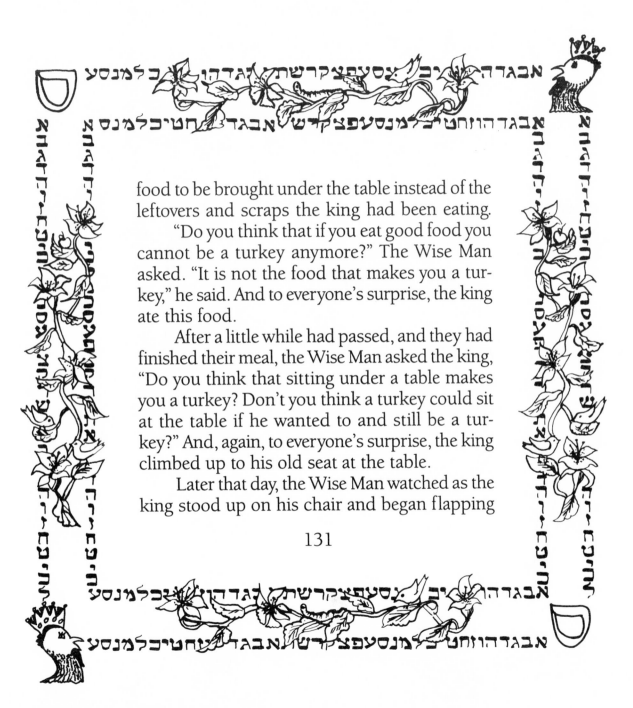

food to be brought under the table instead of the leftovers and scraps the king had been eating.

"Do you think that if you eat good food you cannot be a turkey anymore?" The Wise Man asked. "It is not the food that makes you a turkey," he said. And to everyone's surprise, the king ate this food.

After a little while had passed, and they had finished their meal, the Wise Man asked the king, "Do you think that sitting under a table makes you a turkey? Don't you think a turkey could sit at the table if he wanted to and still be a turkey?" And, again, to everyone's surprise, the king climbed up to his old seat at the table.

Later that day, the Wise Man watched as the king stood up on his chair and began flapping

131

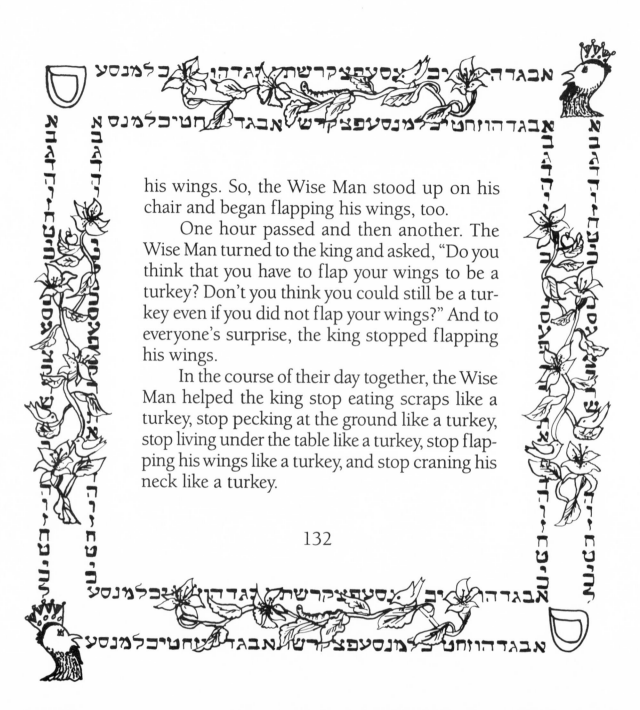

his wings. So, the Wise Man stood up on his chair and began flapping his wings, too.

One hour passed and then another. The Wise Man turned to the king and asked, "Do you think that you have to flap your wings to be a turkey? Don't you think you could still be a turkey even if you did not flap your wings?" And to everyone's surprise, the king stopped flapping his wings.

In the course of their day together, the Wise Man helped the king stop eating scraps like a turkey, stop pecking at the ground like a turkey, stop living under the table like a turkey, stop flapping his wings like a turkey, and stop craning his neck like a turkey.

132

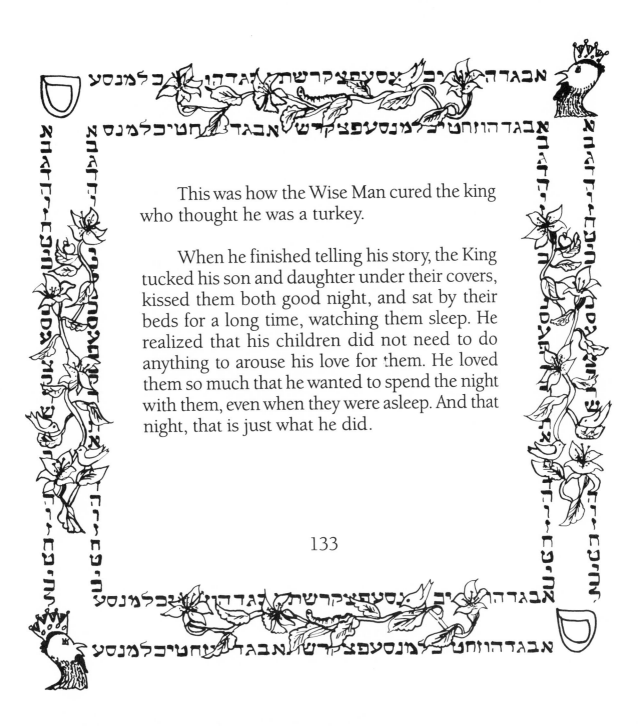

This was how the Wise Man cured the king who thought he was a turkey.

When he finished telling his story, the King tucked his son and daughter under their covers, kissed them both good night, and sat by their beds for a long time, watching them sleep. He realized that his children did not need to do anything to arouse his love for them. He loved them so much that he wanted to spend the night with them, even when they were asleep. And that night, that is just what he did.

*What Is Above
Is Also Below*

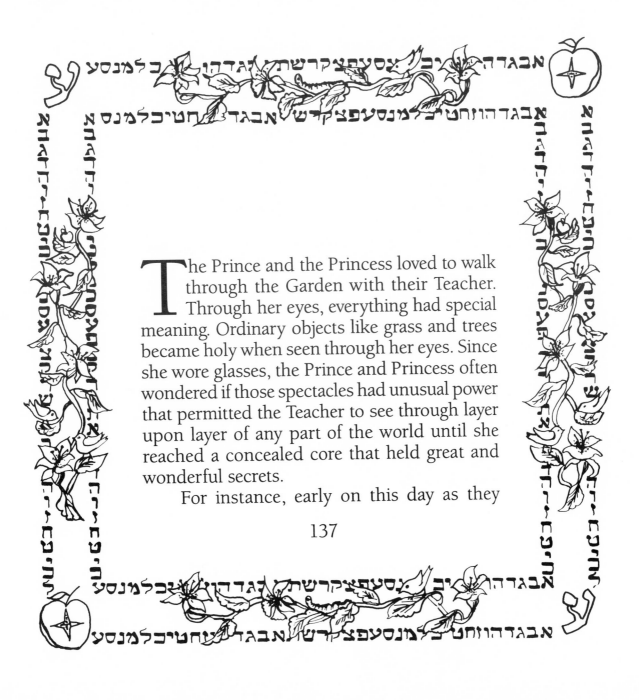

The Prince and the Princess loved to walk through the Garden with their Teacher. Through her eyes, everything had special meaning. Ordinary objects like grass and trees became holy when seen through her eyes. Since she wore glasses, the Prince and Princess often wondered if those spectacles had unusual power that permitted the Teacher to see through layer upon layer of any part of the world until she reached a concealed core that held great and wonderful secrets.

For instance, early on this day as they

137

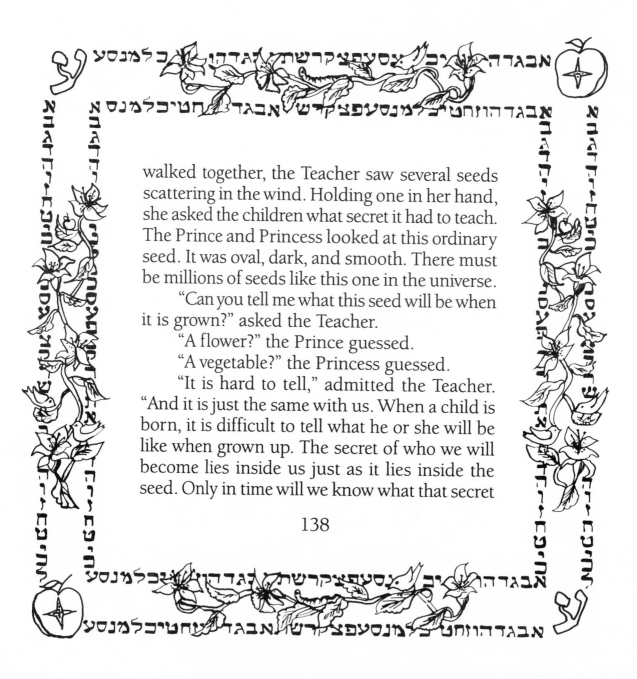

walked together, the Teacher saw several seeds scattering in the wind. Holding one in her hand, she asked the children what secret it had to teach. The Prince and Princess looked at this ordinary seed. It was oval, dark, and smooth. There must be millions of seeds like this one in the universe.

"Can you tell me what this seed will be when it is grown?" asked the Teacher.

"A flower?" the Prince guessed.

"A vegetable?" the Princess guessed.

"It is hard to tell," admitted the Teacher. "And it is just the same with us. When a child is born, it is difficult to tell what he or she will be like when grown up. The secret of who we will become lies inside us just as it lies inside the seed. Only in time will we know what that secret

138

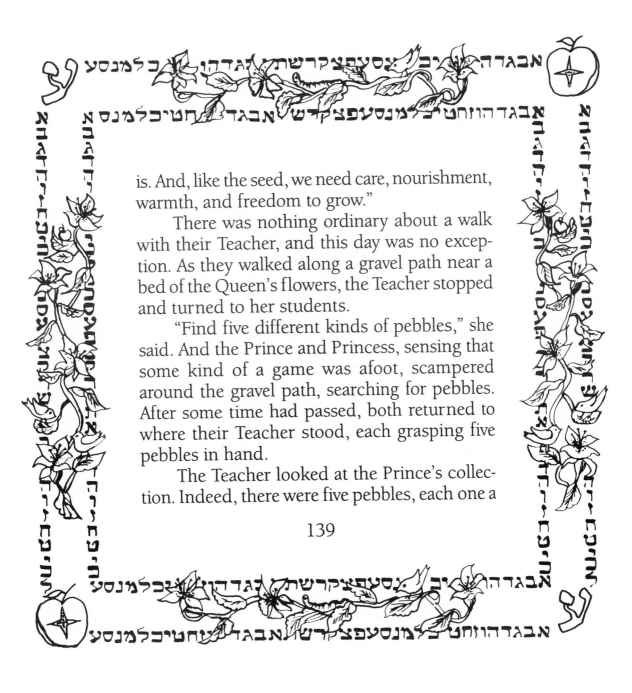

is. And, like the seed, we need care, nourishment, warmth, and freedom to grow."

There was nothing ordinary about a walk with their Teacher, and this day was no exception. As they walked along a gravel path near a bed of the Queen's flowers, the Teacher stopped and turned to her students.

"Find five different kinds of pebbles," she said. And the Prince and Princess, sensing that some kind of a game was afoot, scampered around the gravel path, searching for pebbles. After some time had passed, both returned to where their Teacher stood, each grasping five pebbles in hand.

The Teacher looked at the Prince's collection. Indeed, there were five pebbles, each one a bit different from the next. One was sharper, one was smaller, one was shinier, one was smoother, and one was scratched. The Princess, too, had collected five interesting pebbles. One of hers was pointed, one was almost perfectly round, one was rough, one was white, and one was shaped like a triangle.

"Now," said the Teacher, "put each one back exactly where you found it."

The Prince and Princess looked at each other with expressions of confusion and puzzlement. How were they to put each stone back where it was found? Who could remember something like that? Who paid attention to that kind of detail? Why was it so important?

Then the Teacher picked up a pebble from

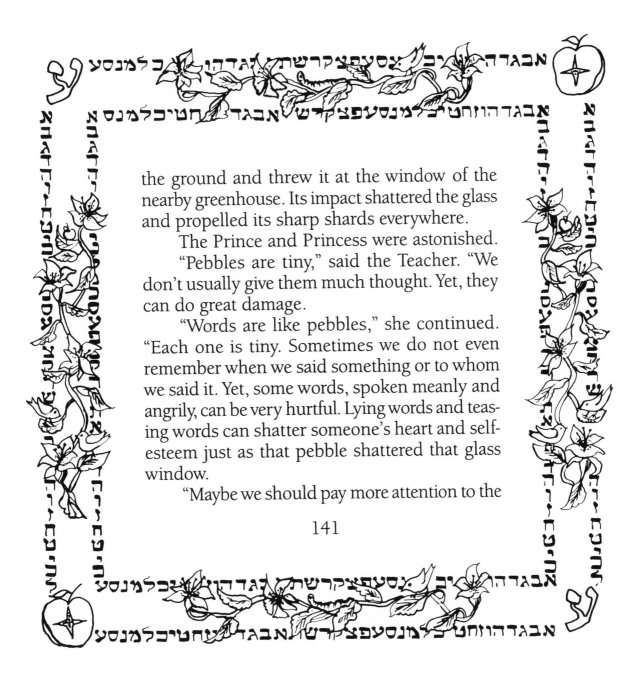

the ground and threw it at the window of the nearby greenhouse. Its impact shattered the glass and propelled its sharp shards everywhere.

The Prince and Princess were astonished.

"Pebbles are tiny," said the Teacher. "We don't usually give them much thought. Yet, they can do great damage.

"Words are like pebbles," she continued. "Each one is tiny. Sometimes we do not even remember when we said something or to whom we said it. Yet, some words, spoken meanly and angrily, can be very hurtful. Lying words and teasing words can shatter someone's heart and self-esteem just as that pebble shattered that glass window.

"Maybe we should pay more attention to the

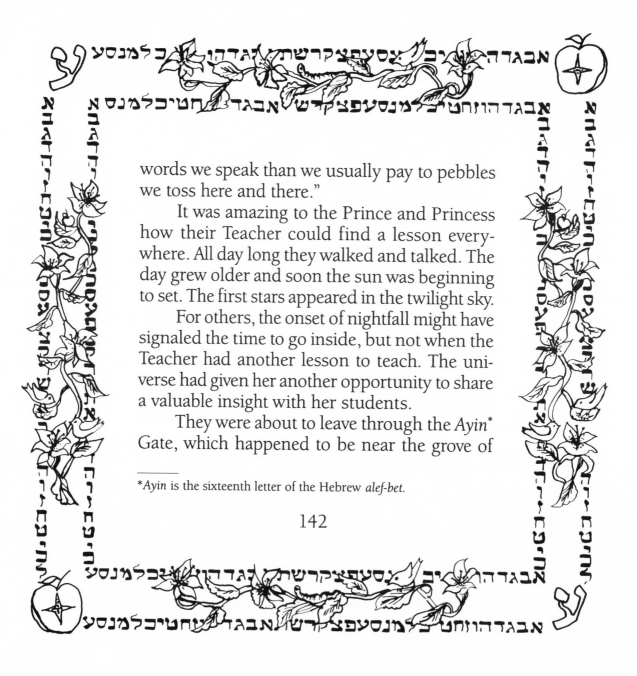

words we speak than we usually pay to pebbles we toss here and there."

It was amazing to the Prince and Princess how their Teacher could find a lesson everywhere. All day long they walked and talked. The day grew older and soon the sun was beginning to set. The first stars appeared in the twilight sky.

For others, the onset of nightfall might have signaled the time to go inside, but not when the Teacher had another lesson to teach. The universe had given her another opportunity to share a valuable insight with her students.

They were about to leave through the *Ayin** Gate, which happened to be near the grove of

---

*Ayin is the sixteenth letter of the Hebrew *alef-bet*.

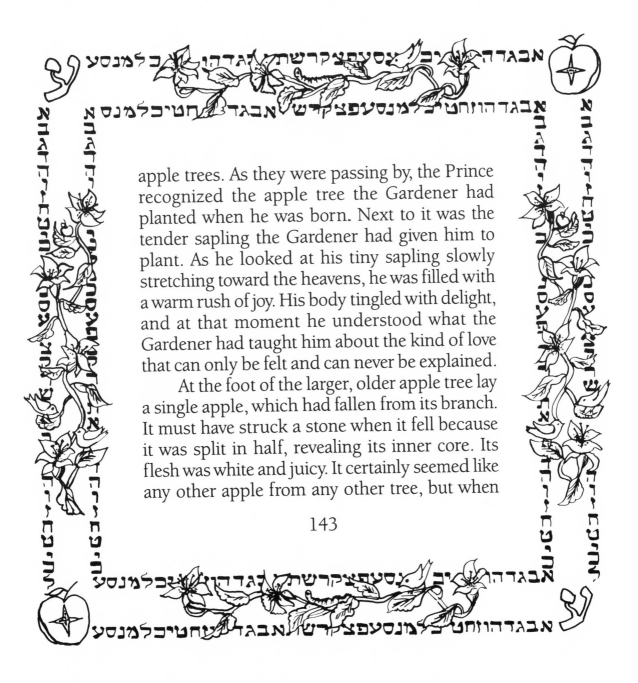

apple trees. As they were passing by, the Prince recognized the apple tree the Gardener had planted when he was born. Next to it was the tender sapling the Gardener had given him to plant. As he looked at his tiny sapling slowly stretching toward the heavens, he was filled with a warm rush of joy. His body tingled with delight, and at that moment he understood what the Gardener had taught him about the kind of love that can only be felt and can never be explained.

At the foot of the larger, older apple tree lay a single apple, which had fallen from its branch. It must have struck a stone when it fell because it was split in half, revealing its inner core. Its flesh was white and juicy. It certainly seemed like any other apple from any other tree, but when

143

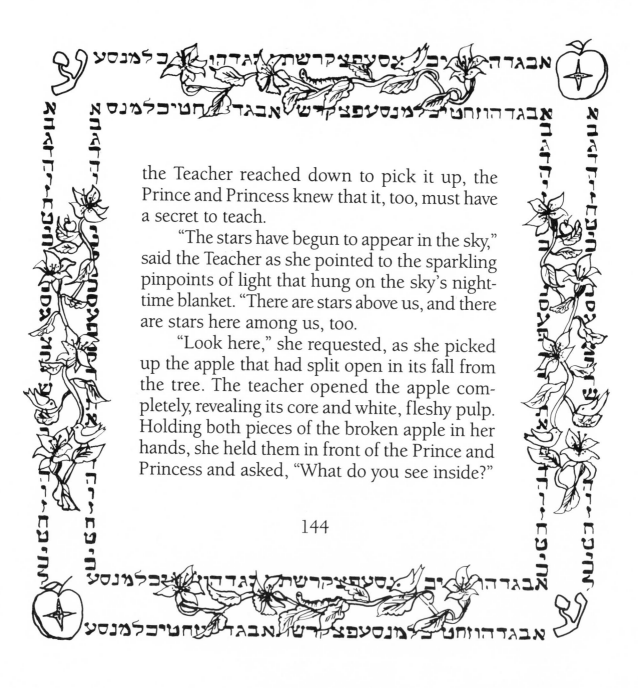

the Teacher reached down to pick it up, the Prince and Princess knew that it, too, must have a secret to teach.

"The stars have begun to appear in the sky," said the Teacher as she pointed to the sparkling pinpoints of light that hung on the sky's nighttime blanket. "There are stars above us, and there are stars here among us, too.

"Look here," she requested, as she picked up the apple that had split open in its fall from the tree. The teacher opened the apple completely, revealing its core and white, fleshy pulp. Holding both pieces of the broken apple in her hands, she held them in front of the Prince and Princess and asked, "What do you see inside?"

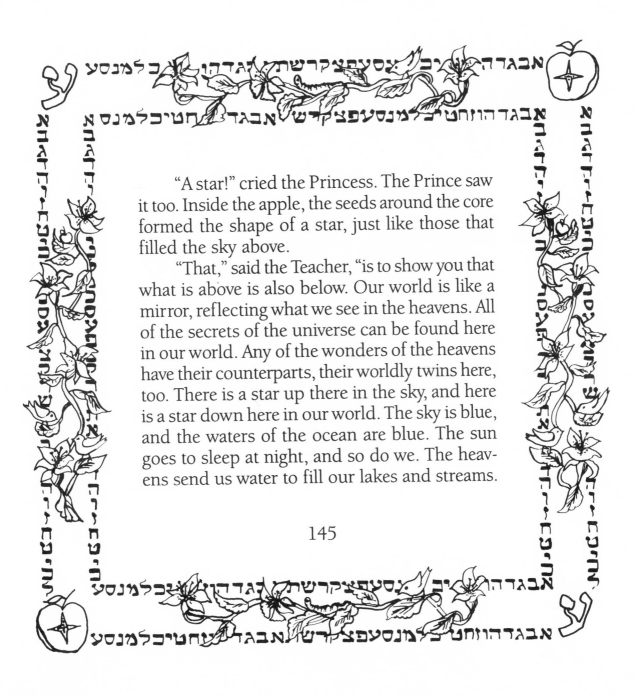

"A star!" cried the Princess. The Prince saw it too. Inside the apple, the seeds around the core formed the shape of a star, just like those that filled the sky above.

"That," said the Teacher, "is to show you that what is above is also below. Our world is like a mirror, reflecting what we see in the heavens. All of the secrets of the universe can be found here in our world. Any of the wonders of the heavens have their counterparts, their worldly twins here, too. There is a star up there in the sky, and here is a star down here in our world. The sky is blue, and the waters of the ocean are blue. The sun goes to sleep at night, and so do we. The heavens send us water to fill our lakes and streams.

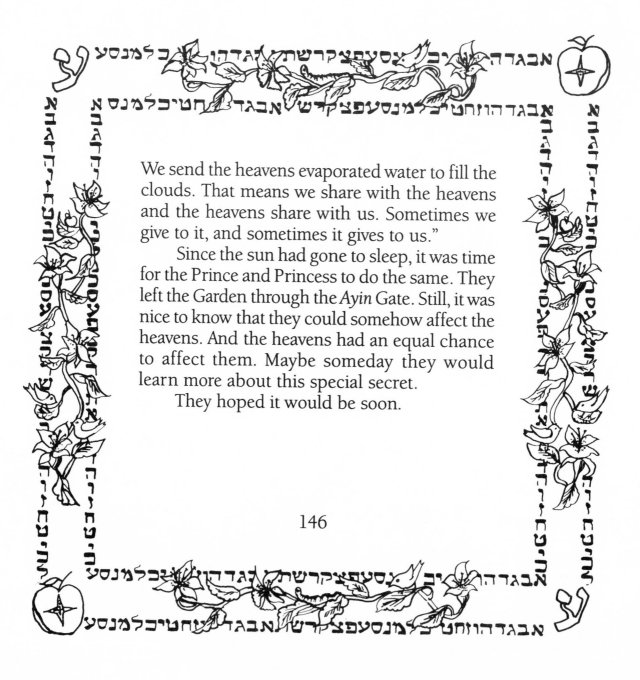

We send the heavens evaporated water to fill the clouds. That means we share with the heavens and the heavens share with us. Sometimes we give to it, and sometimes it gives to us."

Since the sun had gone to sleep, it was time for the Prince and Princess to do the same. They left the Garden through the *Ayin* Gate. Still, it was nice to know that they could somehow affect the heavens. And the heavens had an equal chance to affect them. Maybe someday they would learn more about this special secret.

They hoped it would be soon.

146

*Sometimes You Have to
Do It Yourself*

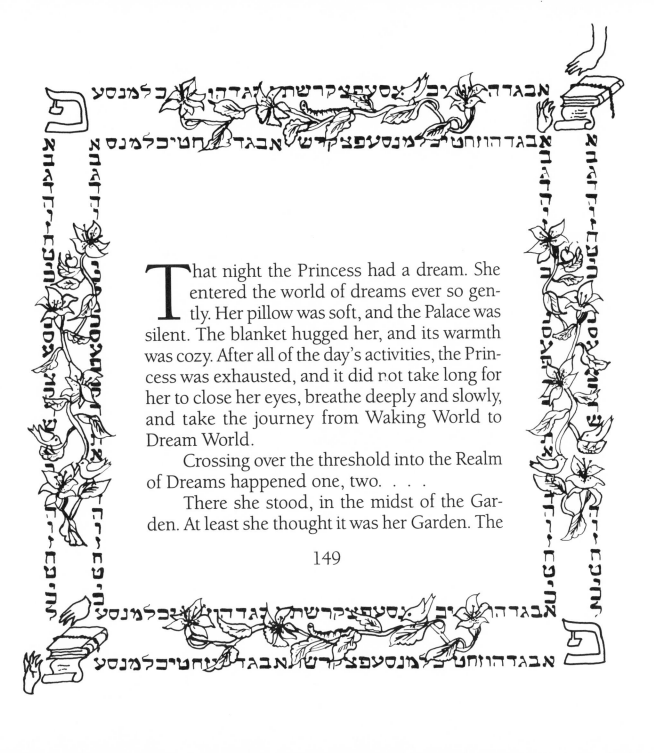

That night the Princess had a dream. She entered the world of dreams ever so gently. Her pillow was soft, and the Palace was silent. The blanket hugged her, and its warmth was cozy. After all of the day's activities, the Princess was exhausted, and it did not take long for her to close her eyes, breathe deeply and slowly, and take the journey from Waking World to Dream World.

Crossing over the threshold into the Realm of Dreams happened one, two. . . .

There she stood, in the midst of the Garden. At least she thought it was her Garden. The

149

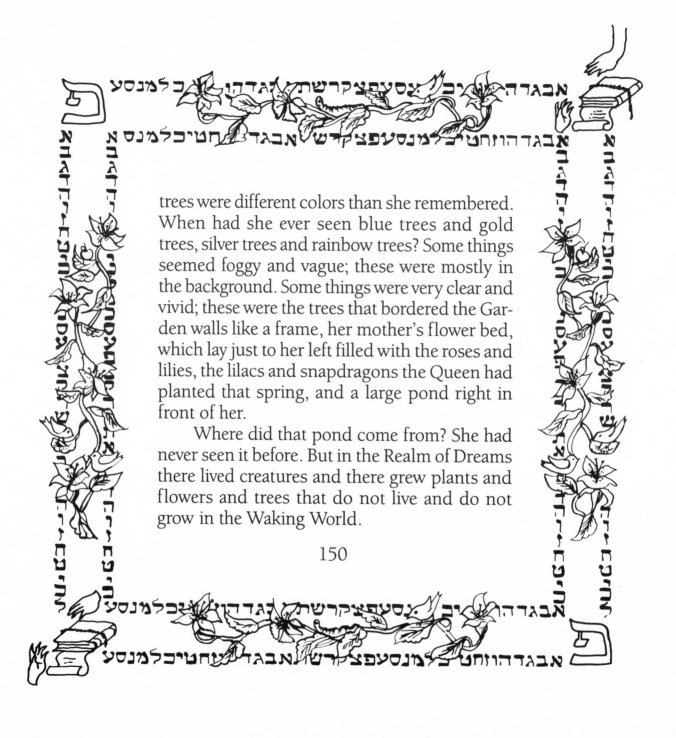

trees were different colors than she remembered. When had she ever seen blue trees and gold trees, silver trees and rainbow trees? Some things seemed foggy and vague; these were mostly in the background. Some things were very clear and vivid; these were the trees that bordered the Garden walls like a frame, her mother's flower bed, which lay just to her left filled with the roses and lilies, the lilacs and snapdragons the Queen had planted that spring, and a large pond right in front of her.

Where did that pond come from? She had never seen it before. But in the Realm of Dreams there lived creatures and there grew plants and flowers and trees that do not live and do not grow in the Waking World.

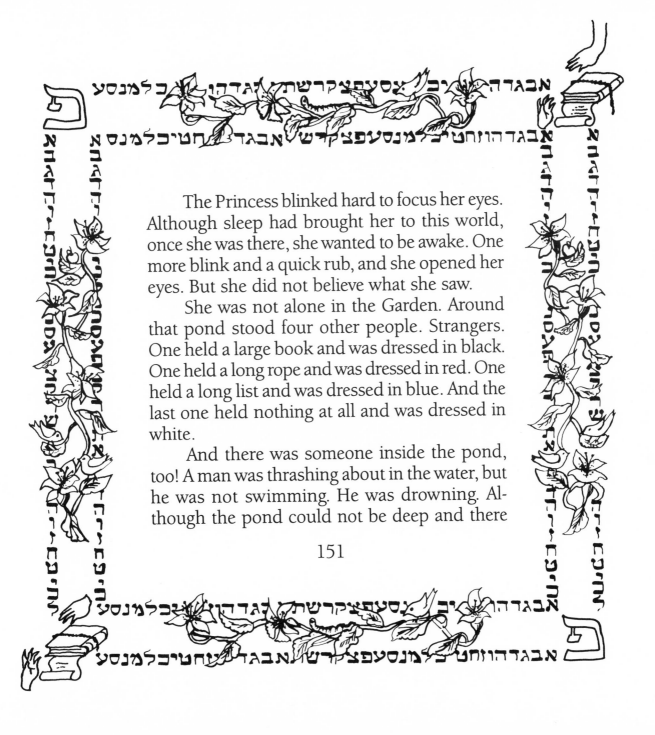

The Princess blinked hard to focus her eyes. Although sleep had brought her to this world, once she was there, she wanted to be awake. One more blink and a quick rub, and she opened her eyes. But she did not believe what she saw.

She was not alone in the Garden. Around that pond stood four other people. Strangers. One held a large book and was dressed in black. One held a long rope and was dressed in red. One held a long list and was dressed in blue. And the last one held nothing at all and was dressed in white.

And there was someone inside the pond, too! A man was thrashing about in the water, but he was not swimming. He was drowning. Although the pond could not be deep and there

151

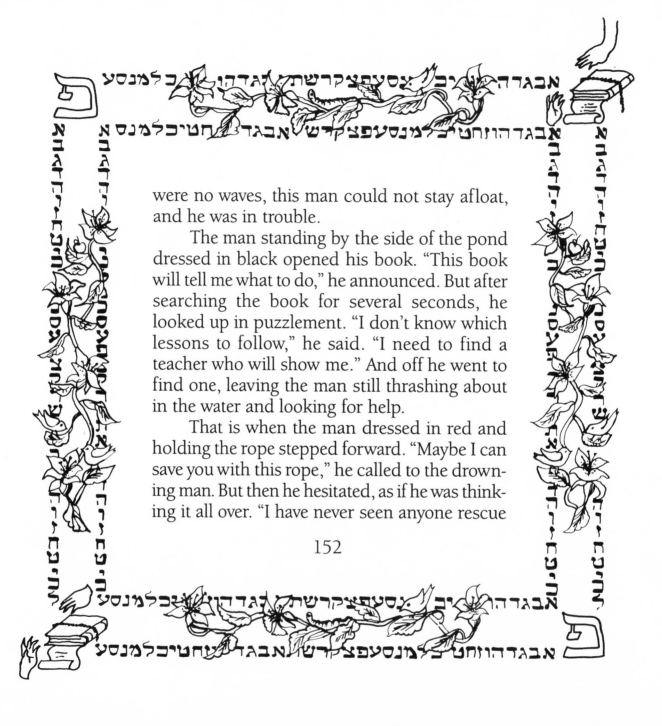

were no waves, this man could not stay afloat, and he was in trouble.

The man standing by the side of the pond dressed in black opened his book. "This book will tell me what to do," he announced. But after searching the book for several seconds, he looked up in puzzlement. "I don't know which lessons to follow," he said. "I need to find a teacher who will show me." And off he went to find one, leaving the man still thrashing about in the water and looking for help.

That is when the man dressed in red and holding the rope stepped forward. "Maybe I can save you with this rope," he called to the drowning man. But then he hesitated, as if he was thinking it all over. "I have never seen anyone rescue

152

a drowning man with a rope before. I think I need to find someone who can show me how to use this rope." And before the drowning man could offer a protest, the man dressed in red was off in search of someone who could show him how to use a rope to save someone who was drowning.

Then the man dressed in blue looked at his list. "Maybe there is something written here I can use to help you," he called to the drowning man. First he looked down the items on the list. Then he looked up the items on the list. He turned the paper over to see if anything was on the back. And he turned the paper back to the front to see if he had missed anything on that side.

"There is nothing on my list to help drown-

153

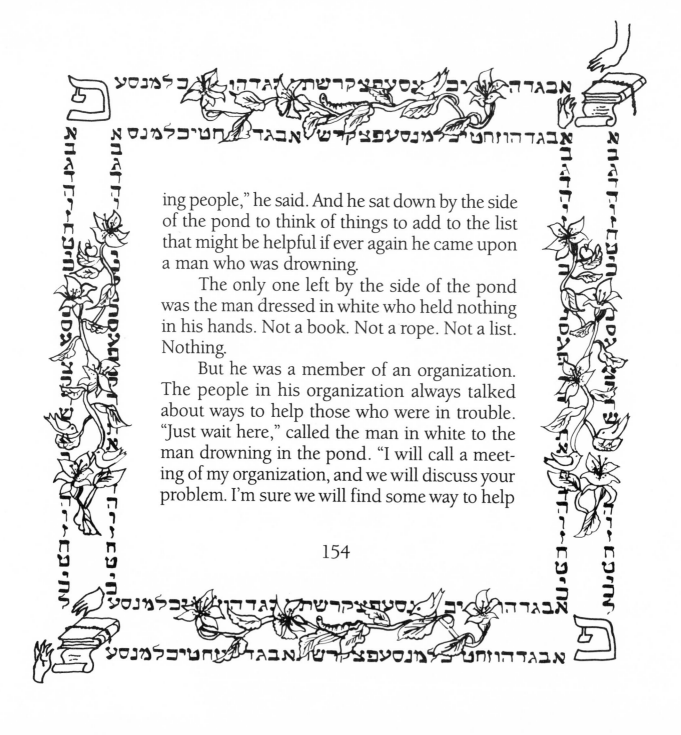

ing people," he said. And he sat down by the side of the pond to think of things to add to the list that might be helpful if ever again he came upon a man who was drowning.

The only one left by the side of the pond was the man dressed in white who held nothing in his hands. Not a book. Not a rope. Not a list. Nothing.

But he was a member of an organization. The people in his organization always talked about ways to help those who were in trouble. "Just wait here," called the man in white to the man drowning in the pond. "I will call a meeting of my organization, and we will discuss your problem. I'm sure we will find some way to help

154

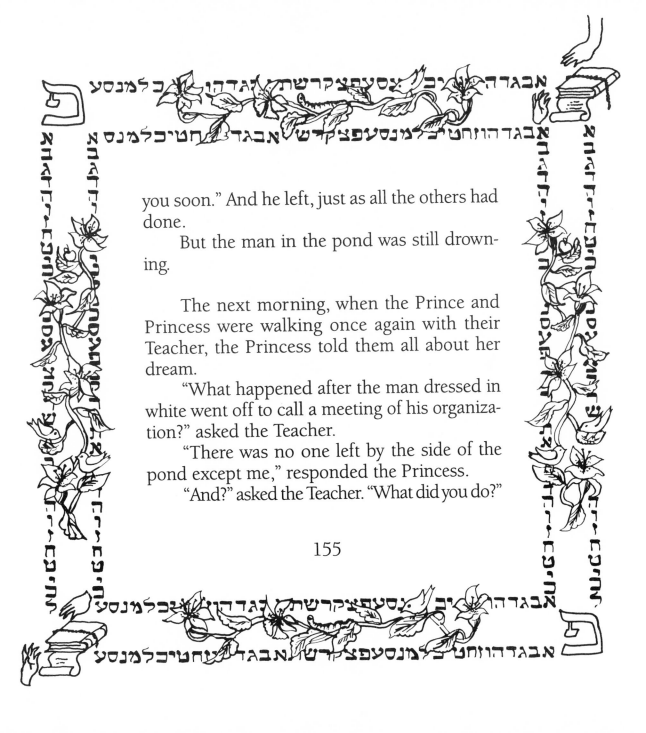

you soon." And he left, just as all the others had done.

But the man in the pond was still drowning.

The next morning, when the Prince and Princess were walking once again with their Teacher, the Princess told them all about her dream.

"What happened after the man dressed in white went off to call a meeting of his organization?" asked the Teacher.

"There was no one left by the side of the pond except me," responded the Princess.

"And?" asked the Teacher. "What did you do?"

155

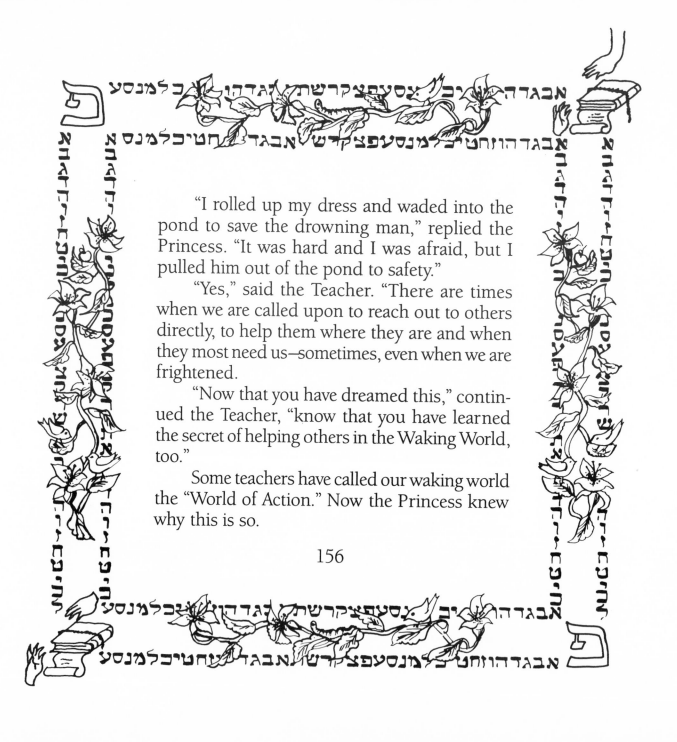

"I rolled up my dress and waded into the pond to save the drowning man," replied the Princess. "It was hard and I was afraid, but I pulled him out of the pond to safety."

"Yes," said the Teacher. "There are times when we are called upon to reach out to others directly, to help them where they are and when they most need us–sometimes, even when we are frightened.

"Now that you have dreamed this," continued the Teacher, "know that you have learned the secret of helping others in the Waking World, too."

Some teachers have called our waking world the "World of Action." Now the Princess knew why this is so.

A Fallen Sparrow

אבגדהוזב שצעהסצקרשת הדהו בלמנסע
אבגדהוזחטיכלמנסעפצקדש אבגד חטיכלמנס

As they entered the *Tzadee** Gate, the Princess was the first to spot something strange on the ground. It was a fallen sparrow. Untouched, but unmoving as well, it lay lifeless upon the ground. Perhaps it had fallen from a branch of the Great Tree, which grew in the middle of the Garden. Perhaps it had flown from a land far away and the exertion of flying such a distance had exhausted it beyond recuperation. Perhaps it had succumbed to any one

---

Tzadee is the eighteenth letter of the Hebrew *alef-bet*.

אבגדהו יב נסעצקרשת בגדהוז בלמנסע
אבגדהוזחט בלמנסעפצקרש אבגד עחטיכלמנסע

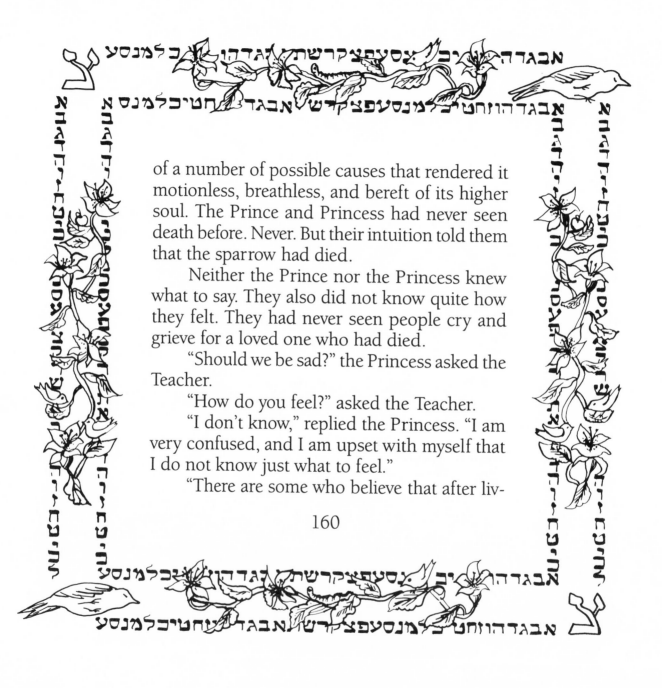

of a number of possible causes that rendered it motionless, breathless, and bereft of its higher soul. The Prince and Princess had never seen death before. Never. But their intuition told them that the sparrow had died.

Neither the Prince nor the Princess knew what to say. They also did not know quite how they felt. They had never seen people cry and grieve for a loved one who had died.

"Should we be sad?" the Princess asked the Teacher.

"How do you feel?" asked the Teacher.

"I don't know," replied the Princess. "I am very confused, and I am upset with myself that I do not know just what to feel."

"There are some who believe that after liv-

160

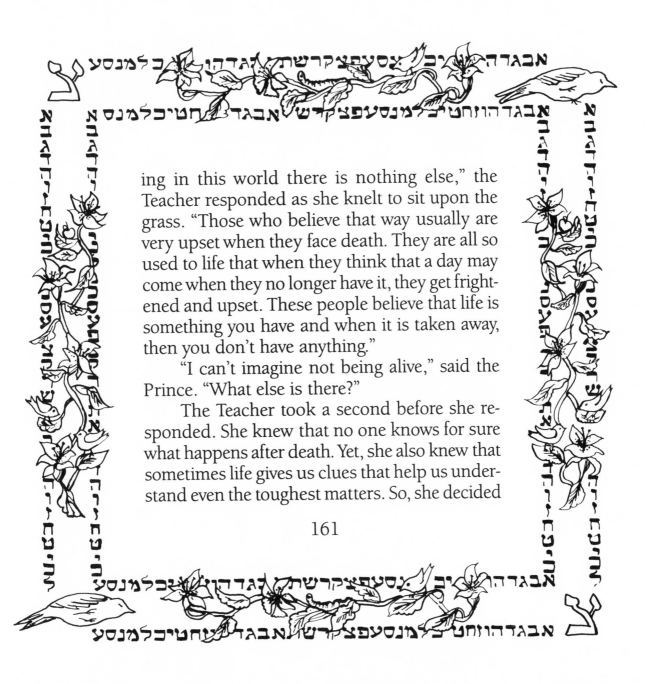

ing in this world there is nothing else," the Teacher responded as she knelt to sit upon the grass. "Those who believe that way usually are very upset when they face death. They are all so used to life that when they think that a day may come when they no longer have it, they get frightened and upset. These people believe that life is something you have and when it is taken away, then you don't have anything."

"I can't imagine not being alive," said the Prince. "What else is there?"

The Teacher took a second before she responded. She knew that no one knows for sure what happens after death. Yet, she also knew that sometimes life gives us clues that help us understand even the toughest matters. So, she decided

161

to share some clues she had found about life and death.

She looked at the Prince and Princess. "Life has hinted to me that we all live in many different kinds of worlds," she said.

"The world we are living in now is what some teachers call the Waking World. Then when we sleep, some part of us lives in the Dream World. Both worlds are real, but they are different. We need our bodies to live in the Waking World, but no one has ever needed a body to live in the Dream World."

The Teacher paused to let the Prince and Princess think a little bit about those two different worlds: the Waking World and the Dream World.

162

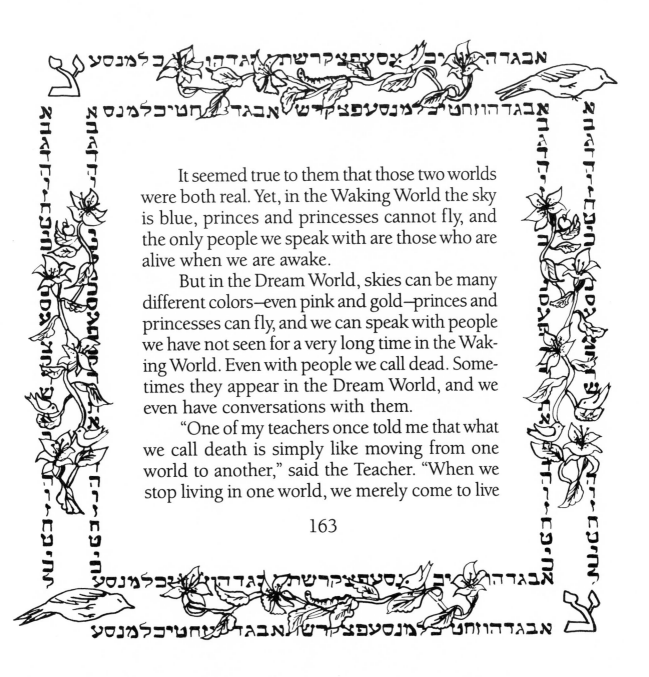

It seemed true to them that those two worlds were both real. Yet, in the Waking World the sky is blue, princes and princesses cannot fly, and the only people we speak with are those who are alive when we are awake.

But in the Dream World, skies can be many different colors–even pink and gold–princes and princesses can fly, and we can speak with people we have not seen for a very long time in the Waking World. Even with people we call dead. Sometimes they appear in the Dream World, and we even have conversations with them.

"One of my teachers once told me that what we call death is simply like moving from one world to another," said the Teacher. "When we stop living in one world, we merely come to live

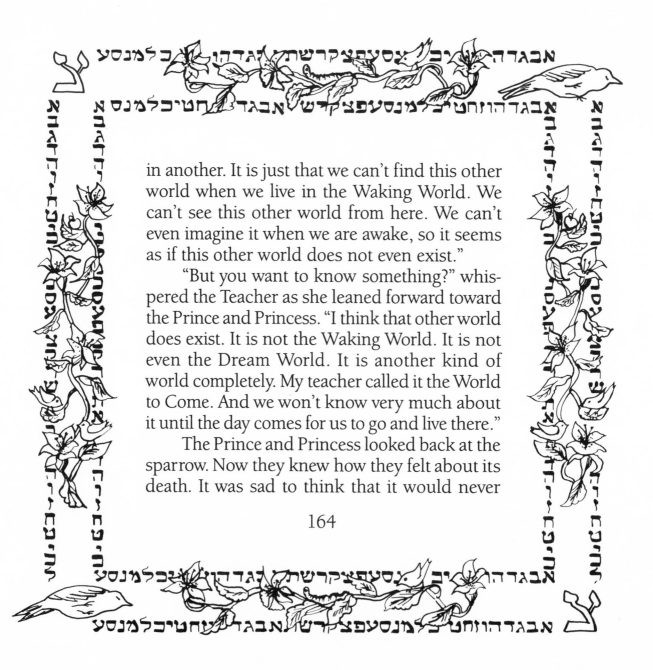

in another. It is just that we can't find this other world when we live in the Waking World. We can't see this other world from here. We can't even imagine it when we are awake, so it seems as if this other world does not even exist."

"But you want to know something?" whispered the Teacher as she leaned forward toward the Prince and Princess. "I think that other world does exist. It is not the Waking World. It is not even the Dream World. It is another kind of world completely. My teacher called it the World to Come. And we won't know very much about it until the day comes for us to go and live there."

The Prince and Princess looked back at the sparrow. Now they knew how they felt about its death. It was sad to think that it would never

164

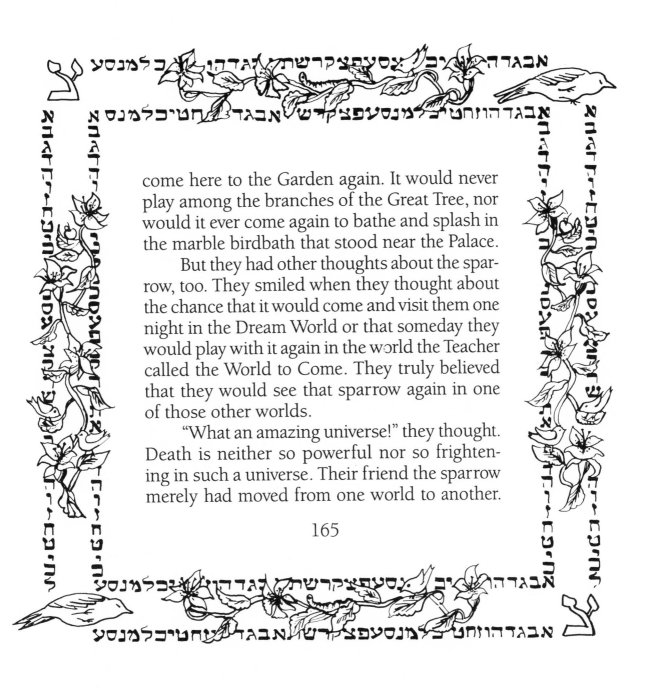

come here to the Garden again. It would never play among the branches of the Great Tree, nor would it ever come again to bathe and splash in the marble birdbath that stood near the Palace.

But they had other thoughts about the sparrow, too. They smiled when they thought about the chance that it would come and visit them one night in the Dream World or that someday they would play with it again in the world the Teacher called the World to Come. They truly believed that they would see that sparrow again in one of those other worlds.

"What an amazing universe!" they thought. Death is neither so powerful nor so frightening in such a universe. Their friend the sparrow merely had moved from one world to another.

165

And speak about moving, the sparrow was not the only one to have moved along. The Prince and Princess noticed that their Teacher had stood up and wandered over to a long-stemmed plant not far away. Another story was about to be revealed.

The Caterpillar's Cocoon

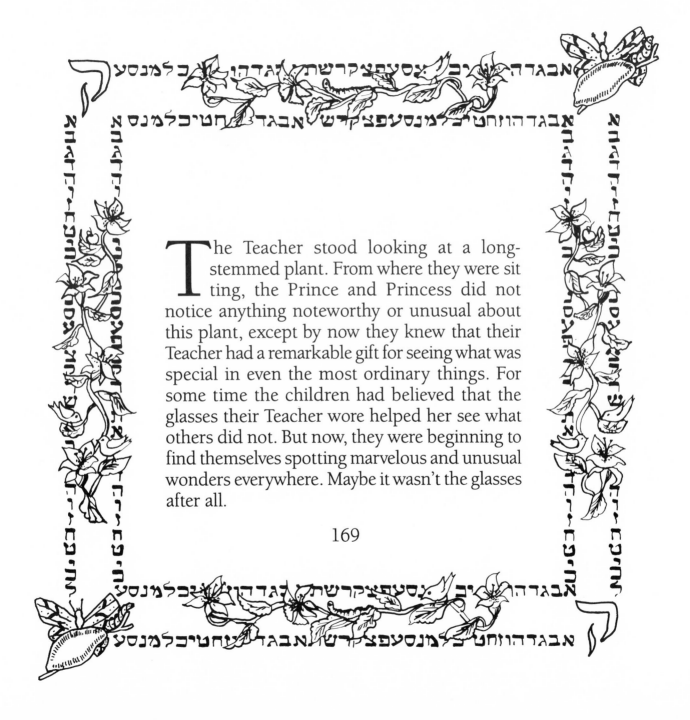

The Teacher stood looking at a long-stemmed plant. From where they were sitting, the Prince and Princess did not notice anything noteworthy or unusual about this plant, except by now they knew that their Teacher had a remarkable gift for seeing what was special in even the most ordinary things. For some time the children had believed that the glasses their Teacher wore helped her see what others did not. But now, they were beginning to find themselves spotting marvelous and unusual wonders everywhere. Maybe it wasn't the glasses after all.

169

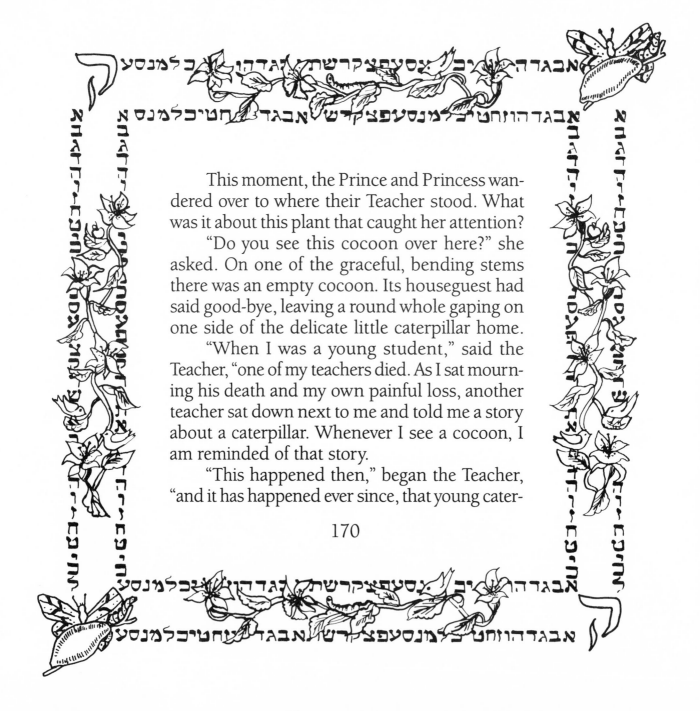

This moment, the Prince and Princess wandered over to where their Teacher stood. What was it about this plant that caught her attention?

"Do you see this cocoon over here?" she asked. On one of the graceful, bending stems there was an empty cocoon. Its houseguest had said good-bye, leaving a round whole gaping on one side of the delicate little caterpillar home.

"When I was a young student," said the Teacher, "one of my teachers died. As I sat mourning his death and my own painful loss, another teacher sat down next to me and told me a story about a caterpillar. Whenever I see a cocoon, I am reminded of that story.

"This happened then," began the Teacher, "and it has happened ever since, that young cater-

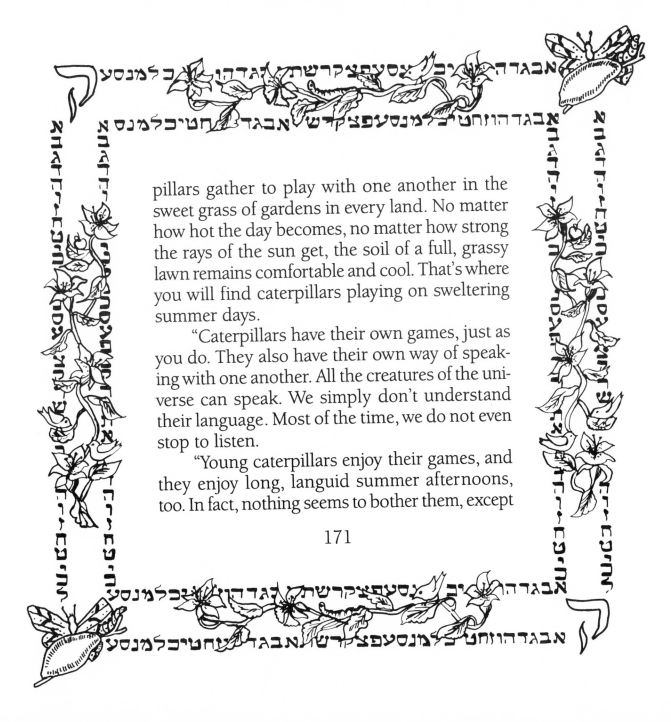

pillars gather to play with one another in the sweet grass of gardens in every land. No matter how hot the day becomes, no matter how strong the rays of the sun get, the soil of a full, grassy lawn remains comfortable and cool. That's where you will find caterpillars playing on sweltering summer days.

"Caterpillars have their own games, just as you do. They also have their own way of speaking with one another. All the creatures of the universe can speak. We simply don't understand their language. Most of the time, we do not even stop to listen.

"Young caterpillars enjoy their games, and they enjoy long, languid summer afternoons, too. In fact, nothing seems to bother them, except

171

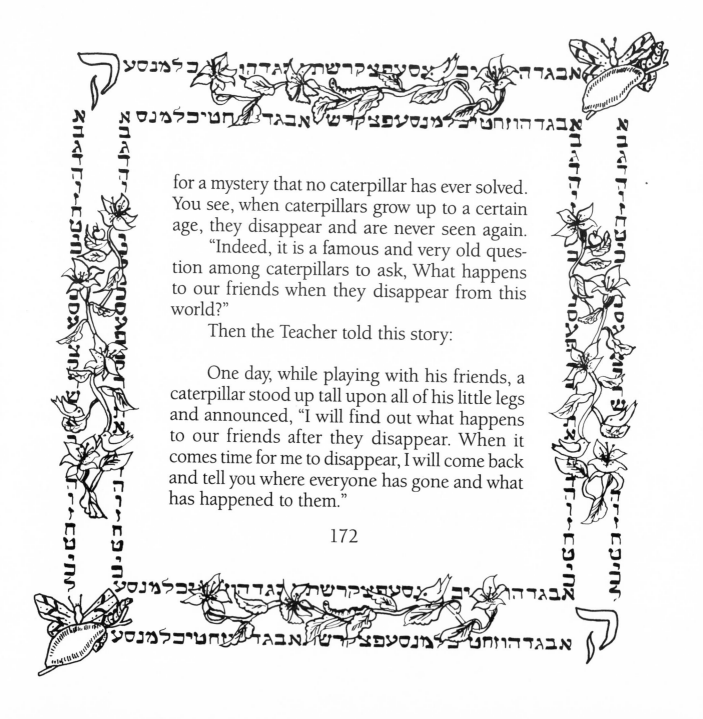

for a mystery that no caterpillar has ever solved. You see, when caterpillars grow up to a certain age, they disappear and are never seen again.

"Indeed, it is a famous and very old question among caterpillars to ask, What happens to our friends when they disappear from this world?"

Then the Teacher told this story:

One day, while playing with his friends, a caterpillar stood up tall upon all of his little legs and announced, "I will find out what happens to our friends after they disappear. When it comes time for me to disappear, I will come back and tell you where everyone has gone and what has happened to them."

172

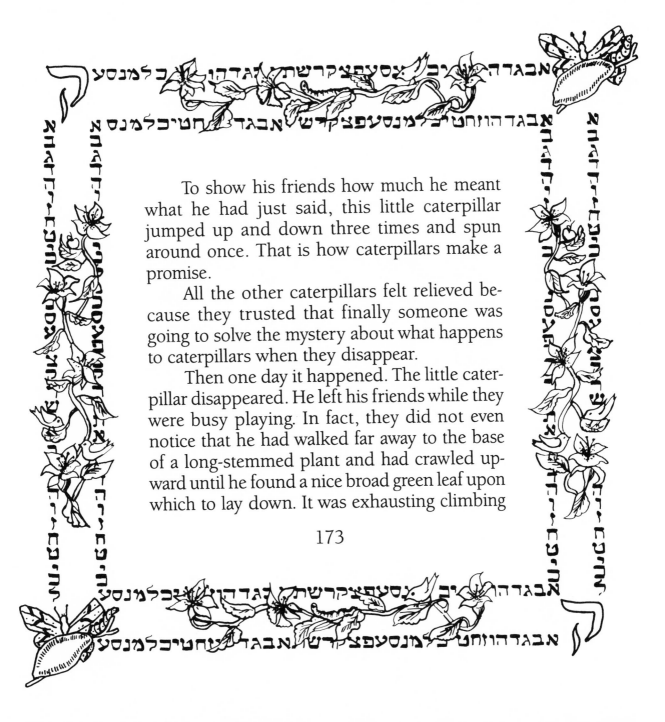

To show his friends how much he meant what he had just said, this little caterpillar jumped up and down three times and spun around once. That is how caterpillars make a promise.

All the other caterpillars felt relieved because they trusted that finally someone was going to solve the mystery about what happens to caterpillars when they disappear.

Then one day it happened. The little caterpillar disappeared. He left his friends while they were busy playing. In fact, they did not even notice that he had walked far away to the base of a long-stemmed plant and had crawled upward until he found a nice broad green leaf upon which to lay down. It was exhausting climbing

173

up so high, but for some reason he felt as if he had to. It was as if he had no choice.

He was so tired. All he wanted to do was sleep, but he didn't sleep. Not right away. Instead he spun a cocoon, oozing thread after sticky thread, until he was covered. It was a home of sorts. While it was very small, it was also very snug and safe. Soon after the cocoon was finished, the caterpillar fell asleep inside.

He slept a long time, until he could sleep no more. It was time to leave the cocoon, and so the little caterpillar pushed and pushed and pushed until he poked a hole in the wall of his temporary home. Finally, after enough poking, the hole was sufficiently large to squeeze through. And out he went. In fact, he fell right

174

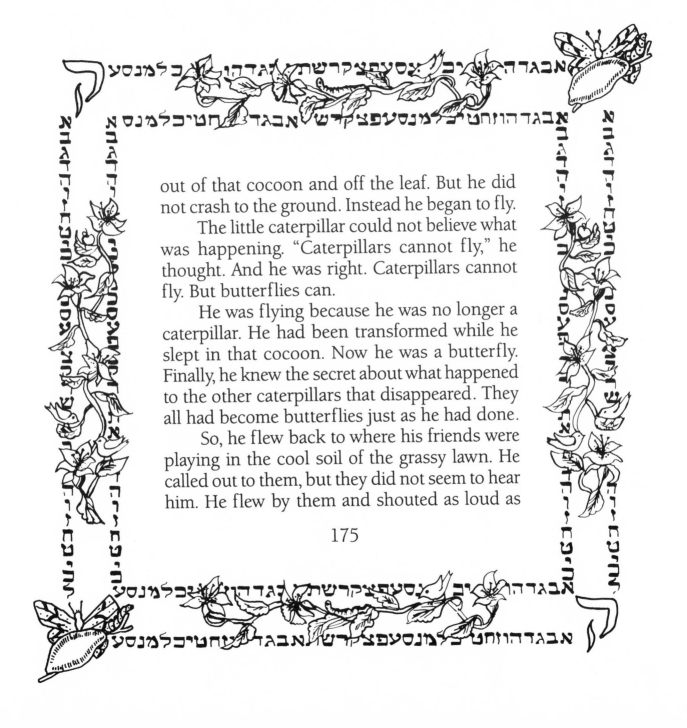

out of that cocoon and off the leaf. But he did not crash to the ground. Instead he began to fly.

The little caterpillar could not believe what was happening. "Caterpillars cannot fly," he thought. And he was right. Caterpillars cannot fly. But butterflies can.

He was flying because he was no longer a caterpillar. He had been transformed while he slept in that cocoon. Now he was a butterfly. Finally, he knew the secret about what happened to the other caterpillars that disappeared. They all had become butterflies just as he had done.

So, he flew back to where his friends were playing in the cool soil of the grassy lawn. He called out to them, but they did not seem to hear him. He flew by them and shouted as loud as

175

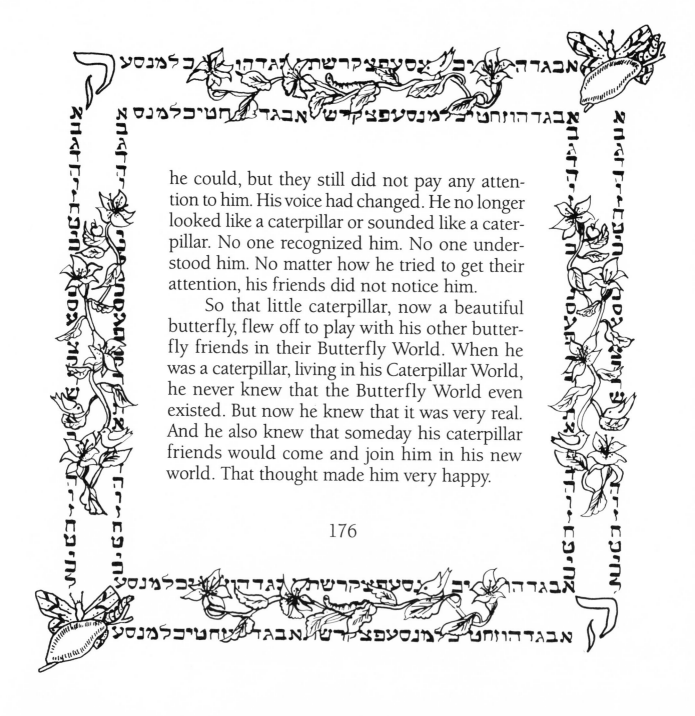

he could, but they still did not pay any attention to him. His voice had changed. He no longer looked like a caterpillar or sounded like a caterpillar. No one recognized him. No one understood him. No matter how he tried to get their attention, his friends did not notice him.

So that little caterpillar, now a beautiful butterfly, flew off to play with his other butterfly friends in their Butterfly World. When he was a caterpillar, living in his Caterpillar World, he never knew that the Butterfly World even existed. But now he knew that it was very real. And he also knew that someday his caterpillar friends would come and join him in his new world. That thought made him very happy.

176

Climbing the Ladder

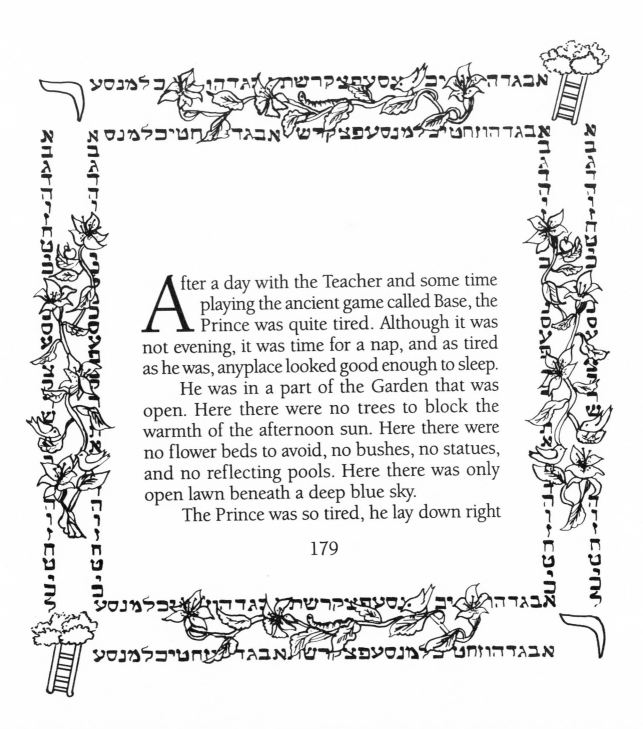

After a day with the Teacher and some time playing the ancient game called Base, the Prince was quite tired. Although it was not evening, it was time for a nap, and as tired as he was, anyplace looked good enough to sleep.

He was in a part of the Garden that was open. Here there were no trees to block the warmth of the afternoon sun. Here there were no flower beds to avoid, no bushes, no statues, and no reflecting pools. Here there was only open lawn beneath a deep blue sky.

The Prince was so tired, he lay down right

179

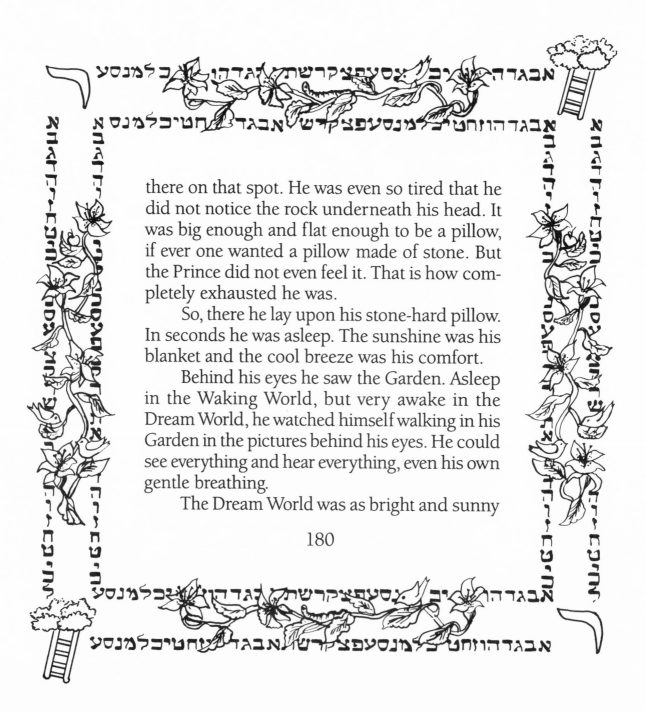

there on that spot. He was even so tired that he did not notice the rock underneath his head. It was big enough and flat enough to be a pillow, if ever one wanted a pillow made of stone. But the Prince did not even feel it. That is how completely exhausted he was.

So, there he lay upon his stone-hard pillow. In seconds he was asleep. The sunshine was his blanket and the cool breeze was his comfort.

Behind his eyes he saw the Garden. Asleep in the Waking World, but very awake in the Dream World, he watched himself walking in his Garden in the pictures behind his eyes. He could see everything and hear everything, even his own gentle breathing.

The Dream World was as bright and sunny

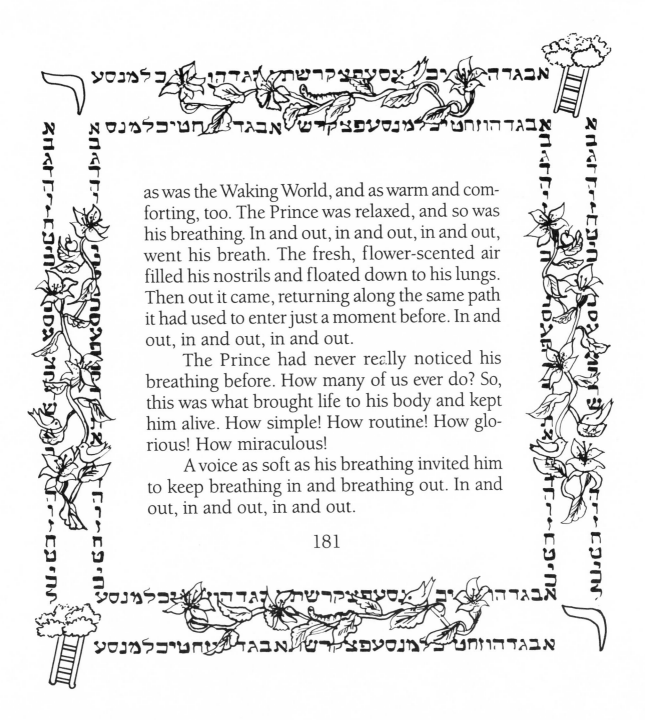

as was the Waking World, and as warm and comforting, too. The Prince was relaxed, and so was his breathing. In and out, in and out, in and out, went his breath. The fresh, flower-scented air filled his nostrils and floated down to his lungs. Then out it came, returning along the same path it had used to enter just a moment before. In and out, in and out, in and out.

The Prince had never really noticed his breathing before. How many of us ever do? So, this was what brought life to his body and kept him alive. How simple! How routine! How glorious! How miraculous!

A voice as soft as his breathing invited him to keep breathing in and breathing out. In and out, in and out, in and out.

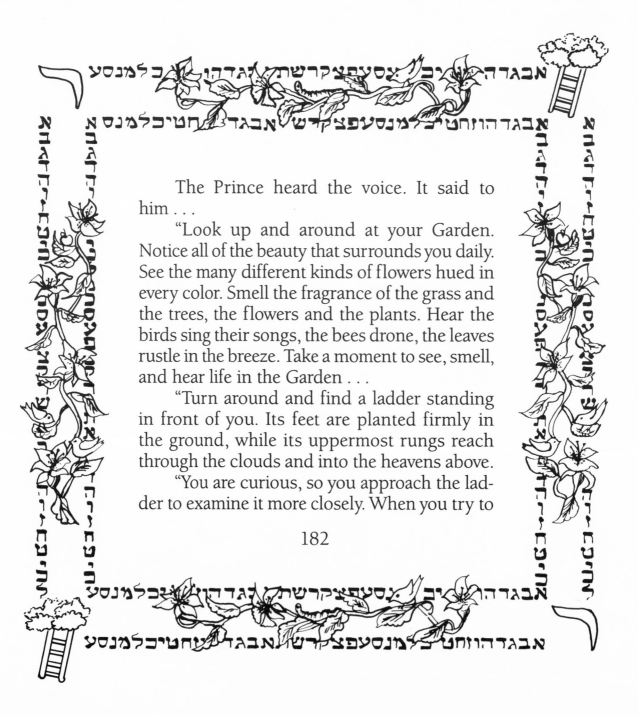

The Prince heard the voice. It said to him . . .

"Look up and around at your Garden. Notice all of the beauty that surrounds you daily. See the many different kinds of flowers hued in every color. Smell the fragrance of the grass and the trees, the flowers and the plants. Hear the birds sing their songs, the bees drone, the leaves rustle in the breeze. Take a moment to see, smell, and hear life in the Garden . . .

"Turn around and find a ladder standing in front of you. Its feet are planted firmly in the ground, while its uppermost rungs reach through the clouds and into the heavens above.

"You are curious, so you approach the ladder to examine it more closely. When you try to

182

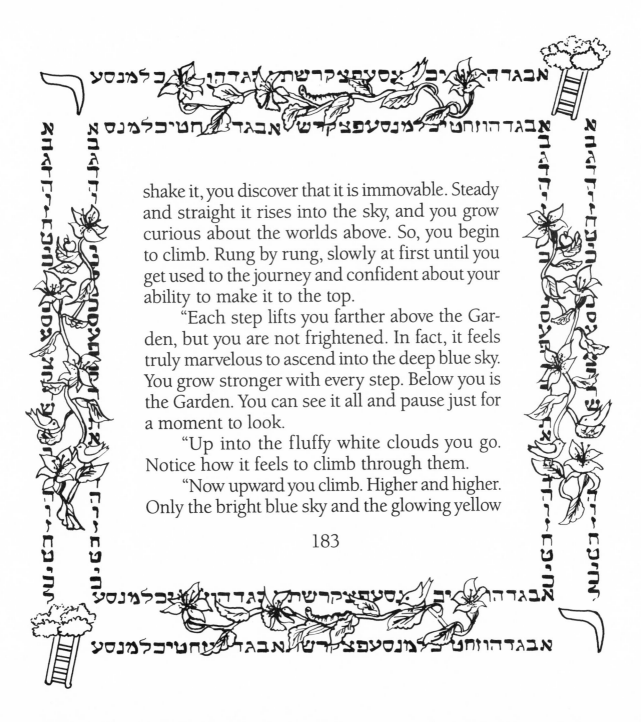

shake it, you discover that it is immovable. Steady and straight it rises into the sky, and you grow curious about the worlds above. So, you begin to climb. Rung by rung, slowly at first until you get used to the journey and confident about your ability to make it to the top.

"Each step lifts you farther above the Garden, but you are not frightened. In fact, it feels truly marvelous to ascend into the deep blue sky. You grow stronger with every step. Below you is the Garden. You can see it all and pause just for a moment to look.

"Up into the fluffy white clouds you go. Notice how it feels to climb through them.

"Now upward you climb. Higher and higher. Only the bright blue sky and the glowing yellow

sun stretch above you. Surrounded by the golden blue light of the heavens, you feel safe and protected. It seems as though that golden blue light illumines you with its glow. Your skin reflects its radiance and glows like the heavens. At this height, your whole body glows with that golden blue light. It makes you feel so alive, so filled with energy, confidence, and joy.

"The heavens glow with golden blue light and you glow, too. From your inside to your outside you glow. Your glow melts into the glow of the heavens until you realize that you are a part of the heavens and they are part of you. You have never felt so wonderful, and you pause to enjoy this feeling. Take all the time you need . . .

184

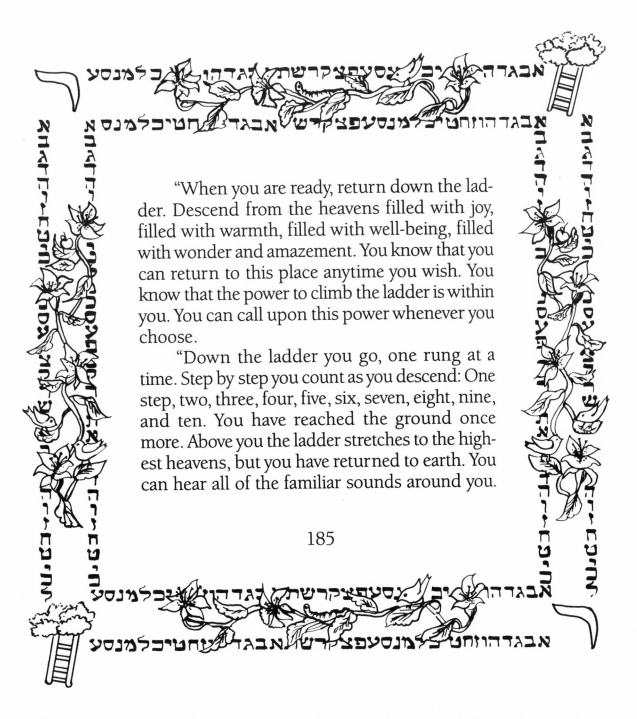

"When you are ready, return down the ladder. Descend from the heavens filled with joy, filled with warmth, filled with well-being, filled with wonder and amazement. You know that you can return to this place anytime you wish. You know that the power to climb the ladder is within you. You can call upon this power whenever you choose.

"Down the ladder you go, one rung at a time. Step by step you count as you descend: One step, two, three, four, five, six, seven, eight, nine, and ten. You have reached the ground once more. Above you the ladder stretches to the highest heavens, but you have returned to earth. You can hear all of the familiar sounds around you.

185

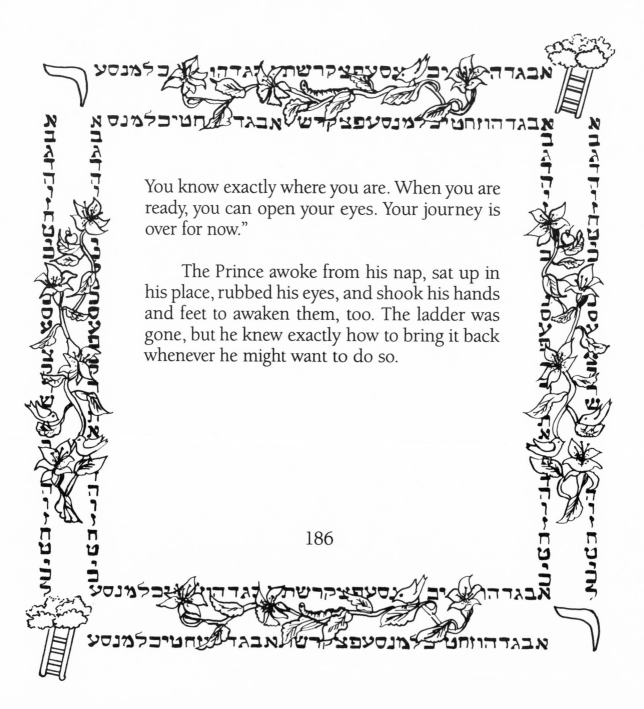

You know exactly where you are. When you are ready, you can open your eyes. Your journey is over for now."

The Prince awoke from his nap, sat up in his place, rubbed his eyes, and shook his hands and feet to awaken them, too. The ladder was gone, but he knew exactly how to bring it back whenever he might want to do so.

186

The Great Bird

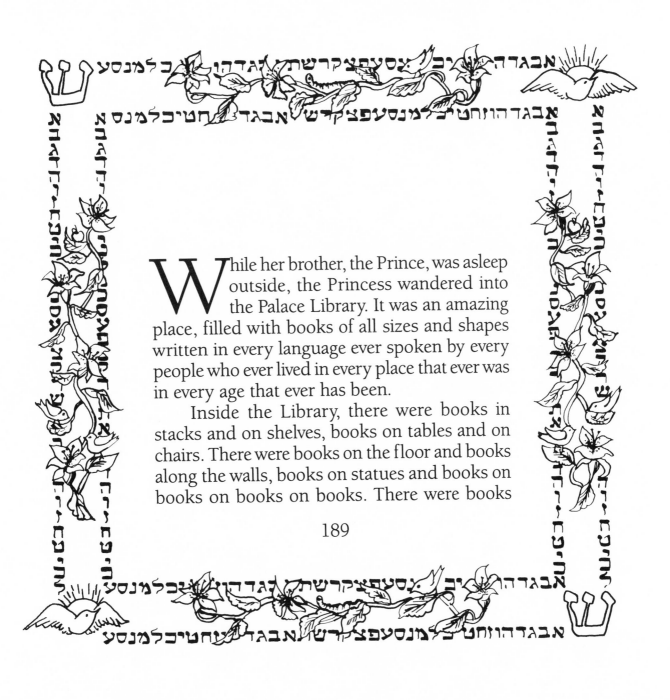

While her brother, the Prince, was asleep outside, the Princess wandered into the Palace Library. It was an amazing place, filled with books of all sizes and shapes written in every language ever spoken by every people who ever lived in every place that ever was in every age that ever has been.

Inside the Library, there were books in stacks and on shelves, books on tables and on chairs. There were books on the floor and books along the walls, books on statues and books on books on books on books. There were books

189

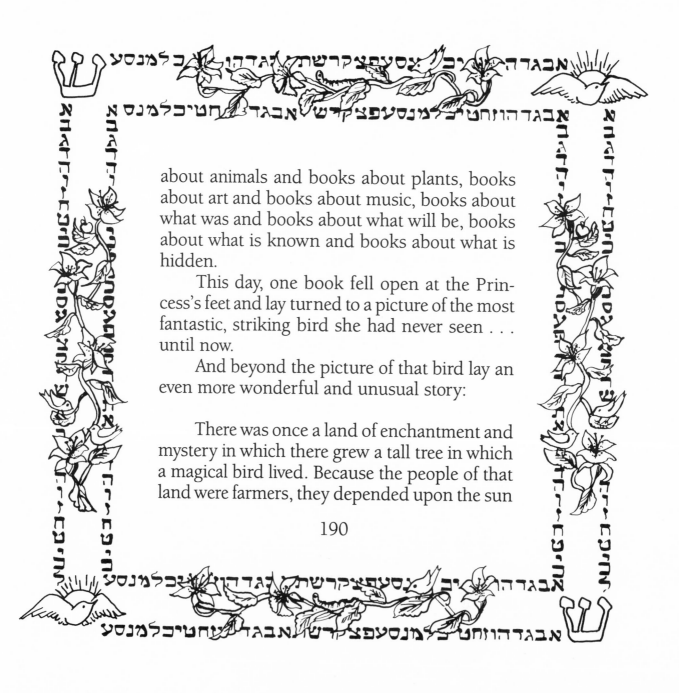

about animals and books about plants, books about art and books about music, books about what was and books about what will be, books about what is known and books about what is hidden.

This day, one book fell open at the Princess's feet and lay turned to a picture of the most fantastic, striking bird she had never seen . . . until now.

And beyond the picture of that bird lay an even more wonderful and unusual story:

There was once a land of enchantment and mystery in which there grew a tall tree in which a magical bird lived. Because the people of that land were farmers, they depended upon the sun

190

to warm the earth and entice the crops to grow and the rain to come and quench their thirst. If there was too much sun, the heat made the crops lazy and languid. So they would droop and sleep rather than stand tall and grow. If there was too much rain, the crops would drown and be washed away. It was best if there was just enough sun and just enough rain.

The Great Bird of the Great Tree made sure that it was so. Her enormous wings would carry her up to the highest clouds. Once there she would tickle the water-laden clouds to release their rain if rain was what the farmers needed. Or, she would flap her wings with such force that the clouds would be blown away to reveal the brilliant sun that shone in their wake.

191

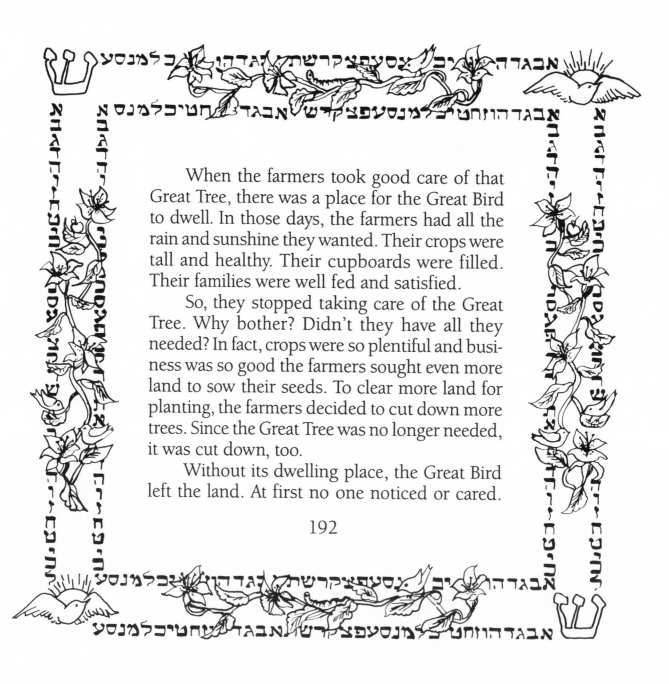

When the farmers took good care of that Great Tree, there was a place for the Great Bird to dwell. In those days, the farmers had all the rain and sunshine they wanted. Their crops were tall and healthy. Their cupboards were filled. Their families were well fed and satisfied.

So, they stopped taking care of the Great Tree. Why bother? Didn't they have all they needed? In fact, crops were so plentiful and business was so good the farmers sought even more land to sow their seeds. To clear more land for planting, the farmers decided to cut down more trees. Since the Great Tree was no longer needed, it was cut down, too.

Without its dwelling place, the Great Bird left the land. At first no one noticed or cared.

192

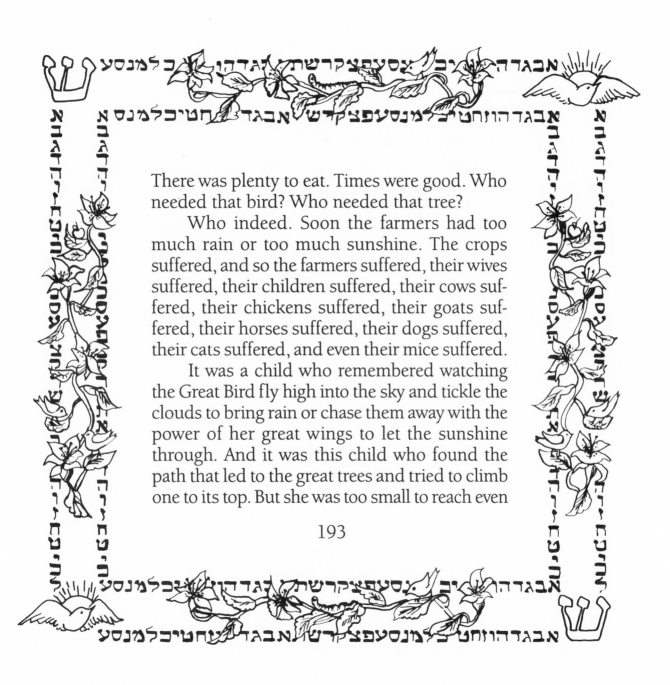

There was plenty to eat. Times were good. Who needed that bird? Who needed that tree?

Who indeed. Soon the farmers had too much rain or too much sunshine. The crops suffered, and so the farmers suffered, their wives suffered, their children suffered, their cows suffered, their chickens suffered, their goats suffered, their horses suffered, their dogs suffered, their cats suffered, and even their mice suffered.

It was a child who remembered watching the Great Bird fly high into the sky and tickle the clouds to bring rain or chase them away with the power of her great wings to let the sunshine through. And it was this child who found the path that led to the great trees and tried to climb one to its top. But she was too small to reach even

193

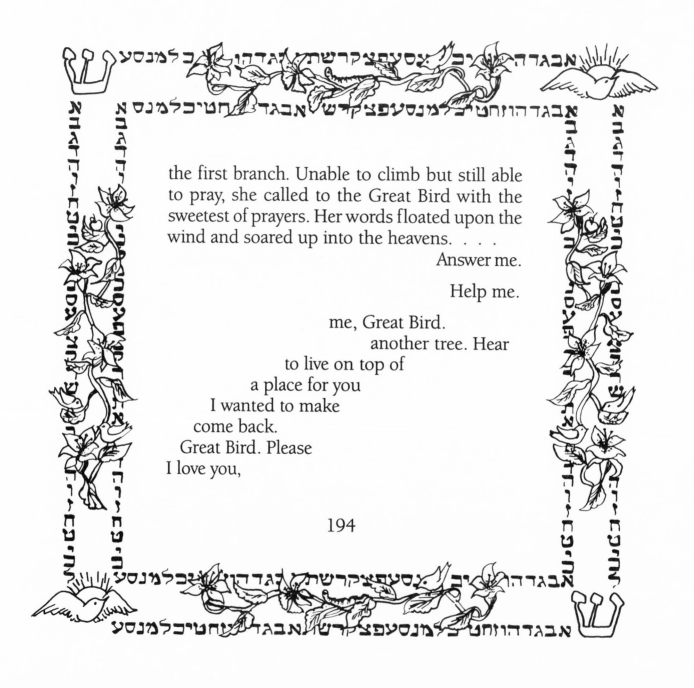

the first branch. Unable to climb but still able to pray, she called to the Great Bird with the sweetest of prayers. Her words floated upon the wind and soared up into the heavens. . . .

Answer me.

Help me.

me, Great Bird.
another tree. Hear
to live on top of
a place for you
I wanted to make
come back.
Great Bird. Please
I love you,

194

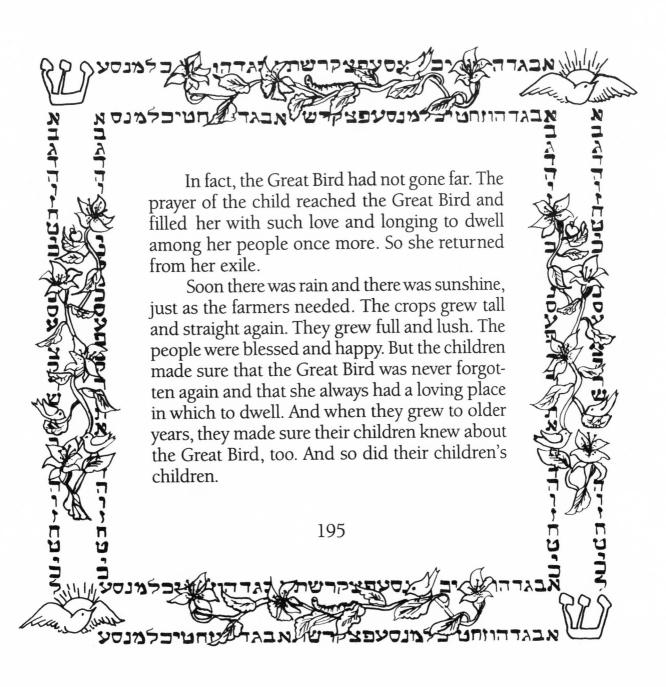

In fact, the Great Bird had not gone far. The prayer of the child reached the Great Bird and filled her with such love and longing to dwell among her people once more. So she returned from her exile.

Soon there was rain and there was sunshine, just as the farmers needed. The crops grew tall and straight again. They grew full and lush. The people were blessed and happy. But the children made sure that the Great Bird was never forgotten again and that she always had a loving place in which to dwell. And when they grew to older years, they made sure their children knew about the Great Bird, too. And so did their children's children.

195

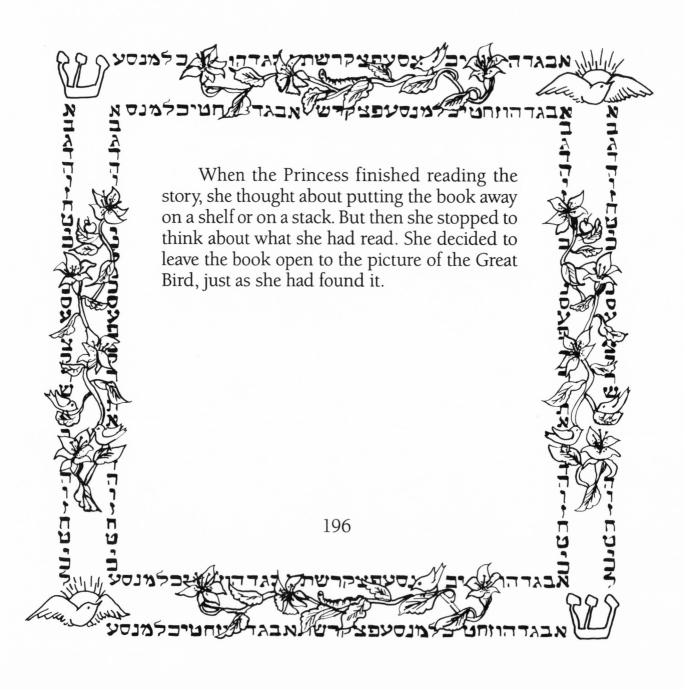

When the Princess finished reading the story, she thought about putting the book away on a shelf or on a stack. But then she stopped to think about what she had read. She decided to leave the book open to the picture of the Great Bird, just as she had found it.

196

The Magic of Old Tales

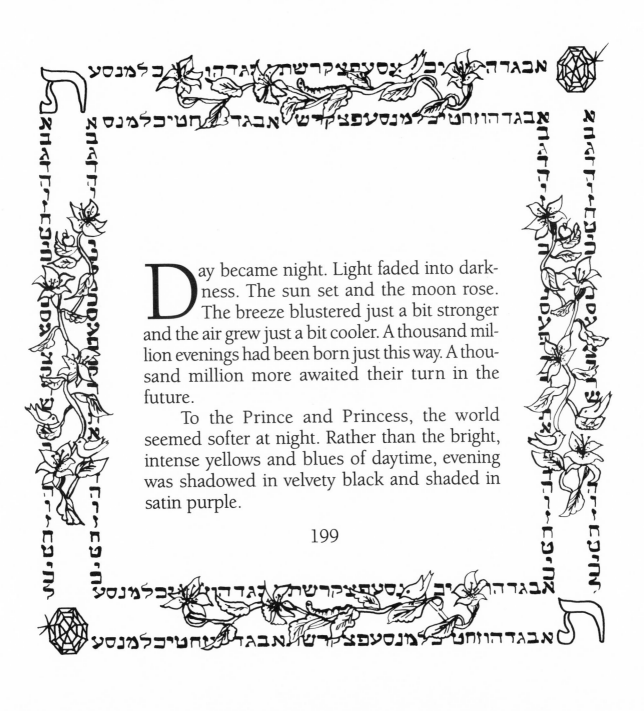

Day became night. Light faded into darkness. The sun set and the moon rose. The breeze blustered just a bit stronger and the air grew just a bit cooler. A thousand million evenings had been born just this way. A thousand million more awaited their turn in the future.

To the Prince and Princess, the world seemed softer at night. Rather than the bright, intense yellows and blues of daytime, evening was shadowed in velvety black and shaded in satin purple.

199

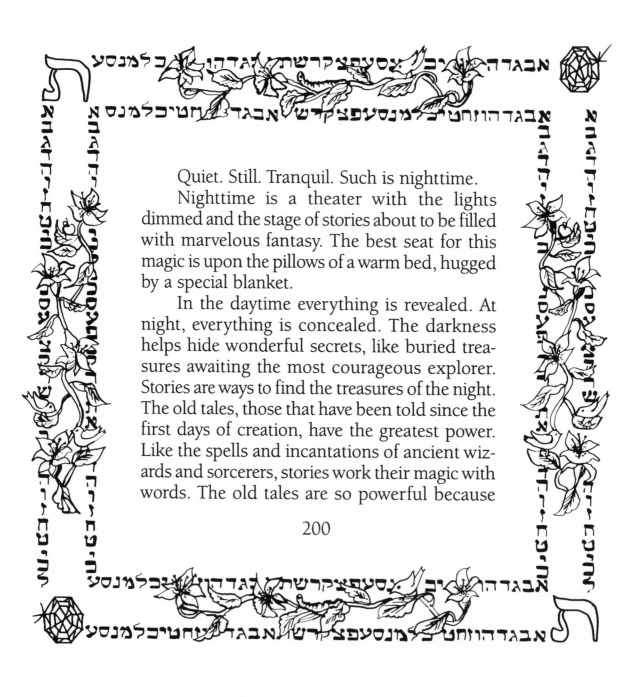

Quiet. Still. Tranquil. Such is nighttime.

Nighttime is a theater with the lights dimmed and the stage of stories about to be filled with marvelous fantasy. The best seat for this magic is upon the pillows of a warm bed, hugged by a special blanket.

In the daytime everything is revealed. At night, everything is concealed. The darkness helps hide wonderful secrets, like buried treasures awaiting the most courageous explorer. Stories are ways to find the treasures of the night. The old tales, those that have been told since the first days of creation, have the greatest power. Like the spells and incantations of ancient wizards and sorcerers, stories work their magic with words. The old tales are so powerful because

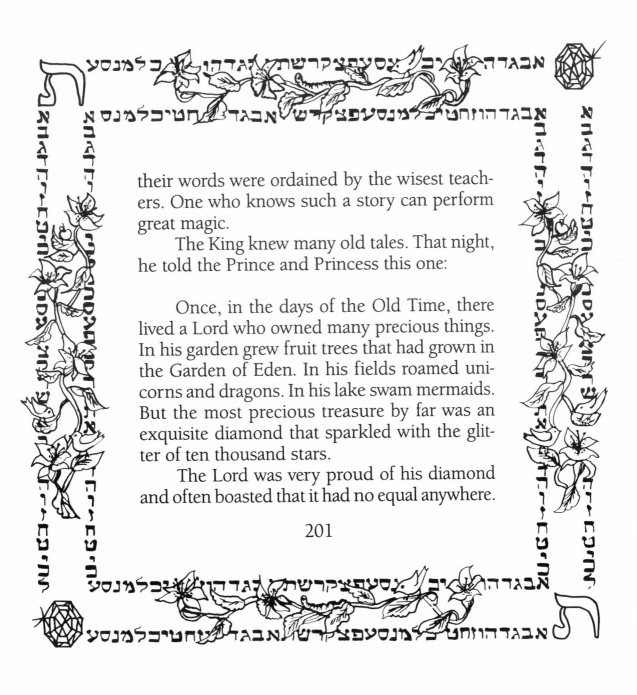

their words were ordained by the wisest teachers. One who knows such a story can perform great magic.

The King knew many old tales. That night, he told the Prince and Princess this one:

Once, in the days of the Old Time, there lived a Lord who owned many precious things. In his garden grew fruit trees that had grown in the Garden of Eden. In his fields roamed unicorns and dragons. In his lake swam mermaids. But the most precious treasure by far was an exquisite diamond that sparkled with the glitter of ten thousand stars.

The Lord was very proud of his diamond and often boasted that it had no equal anywhere.

201

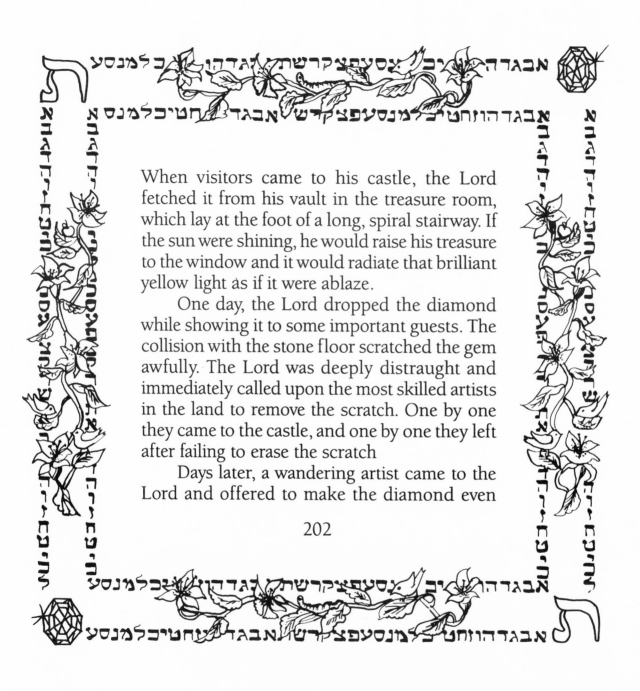

When visitors came to his castle, the Lord fetched it from his vault in the treasure room, which lay at the foot of a long, spiral stairway. If the sun were shining, he would raise his treasure to the window and it would radiate that brilliant yellow light as if it were ablaze.

One day, the Lord dropped the diamond while showing it to some important guests. The collision with the stone floor scratched the gem awfully. The Lord was deeply distraught and immediately called upon the most skilled artists in the land to remove the scratch. One by one they came to the castle, and one by one they left after failing to erase the scratch

Days later, a wandering artist came to the Lord and offered to make the diamond even

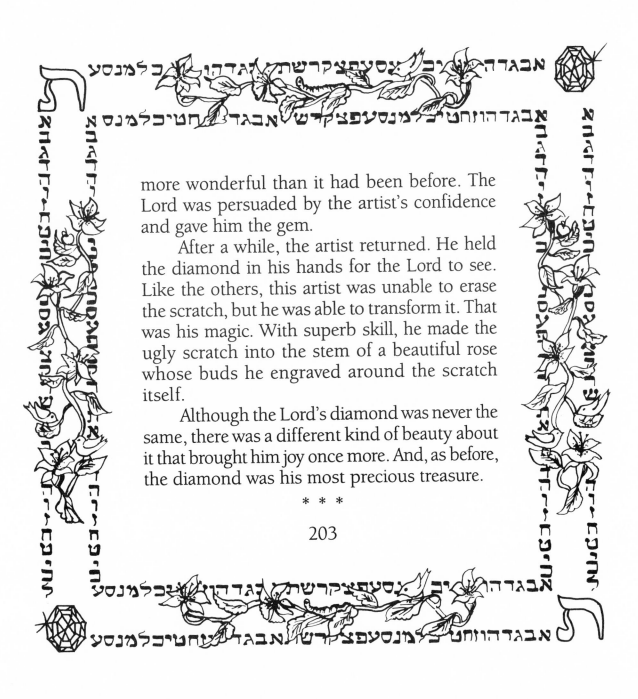

more wonderful than it had been before. The Lord was persuaded by the artist's confidence and gave him the gem.

After a while, the artist returned. He held the diamond in his hands for the Lord to see. Like the others, this artist was unable to erase the scratch, but he was able to transform it. That was his magic. With superb skill, he made the ugly scratch into the stem of a beautiful rose whose buds he engraved around the scratch itself.

Although the Lord's diamond was never the same, there was a different kind of beauty about it that brought him joy once more. And, as before, the diamond was his most precious treasure.

* * *

203

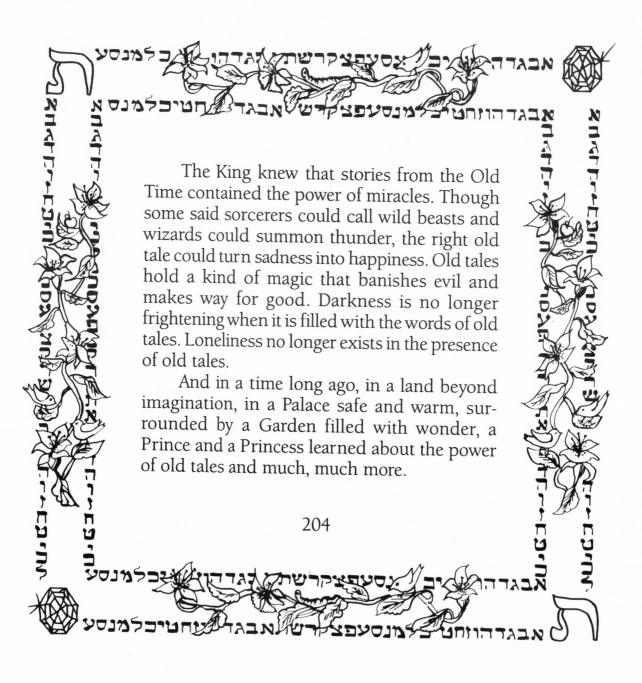

The King knew that stories from the Old Time contained the power of miracles. Though some said sorcerers could call wild beasts and wizards could summon thunder, the right old tale could turn sadness into happiness. Old tales hold a kind of magic that banishes evil and makes way for good. Darkness is no longer frightening when it is filled with the words of old tales. Loneliness no longer exists in the presence of old tales.

And in a time long ago, in a land beyond imagination, in a Palace safe and warm, surrounded by a Garden filled with wonder, a Prince and a Princess learned about the power of old tales and much, much more.

Notes

A Bedtime Story: This tale is based on the rabbinic tale of "Honi the Circle Drawer," found in the Babylonian Talmud, *Taanit* 23a.

If You Think You Are a Chicken: This is my version of a parable I have heard from many different teachers in many different versions. My guess is that they heard it from many different teachers in many different versions, as well. And, I imagine, so it was heard since time began.

A Dream Uninterpreted Is Like a Treasure Unopened:
This title is based on the kabbalistic maxim that a dream uninterpreted is like a letter unread (Babylonian Talmud, *Berachot* 55a). The story itself is based upon a tale that I have heard in various forms since my childhood and that storytellers like Ellen Frankel trace to chasidic origins (*The Classic Tales* [Northvale, NJ: Jason Aronson, 1989], p. 628 n. 264).

The Opal: The story of the opal was inspired by a tale I heard from Rabbi Richard Sherwin of Beth El Congregation in Phoenix, Arizona.

The Inheritance: My wife's mother used *Rozhinkes mit Mandlen* as a lullaby and sang it to my wife in her childhood. My wife used it the same way when she sang it to our daughter, Mikki, in her earliest infancy.

In this story I am employing the kabbalistic principle of *temurah* or "permutation of letters" to reveal that the word *shirah* or "song" and *yerushah* are related on a secret level. The Hebrew characters make this *temurah* evident: שירה becomes ירשה when the consonants are rearranged. *Temurah* was a very popular means used by some kabbalists to uncover mystical relations between one word or concept and another. The example presented here is only one form of *temurah*. Historically, there were many kinds of *temurah* used by the kabbalists.

The King Who Thought He Was a Turkey: This is my version of a famous tale told by R. Nachman of Bratslav (d. 1810). R. Nachman was the great-grandson of the Baal Shem Tov, the founder of modern Chasidism, and a renowned teacher, healer, and *tzaddik* in his own right.

What Is Above Is Also Below: The core of this story is inspired by and based upon a tale entitled "The Apple Tree's Discovery," by Peninnah Schram and Rachayl Eckstein Davis.

Sometimes You Have to Do It Yourself: In the Jewish mystical scheme, the "World of Action," or *Asiyah* in Hebrew, is the lowest of four universes. It is the universe we inhabit, and for many it is the only universe they shall ever come to know in their lifetime. It is characterized, in part, by the existence and predominance of matter as opposed to spirit, its obedience to what are commonly called the physical laws of the universe, and its dependence upon coordinates of space and time for meaning and context.

A Fallen Sparrow: "Moving from one world to another" is my rephrasing of a teaching of the great chasidic teacher Menachem Mendel of Kotzk (d. 1859), who is also known to us as the Kotzker Rebbe. The quote actually attributed to the Kotzker Rebbe is "Death is merely moving from one home to another."

208

The Caterpillar's Cocoon: This story is based upon my stories "Goobi the Grub," in *Sidra Stories: A Torah Companion* (New York: UAHC Press, 1989), and *Deena the Damselfly* (New York: UAHC Press, 1992).

The Magic of Old Tales: The story of the diamond is based upon a parable told by the Dubner *Maggid*. A *maggid* was an itinerant preacher who often used stories and parables to convey wisdom and Torah. The Dubner *Maggid* (d. 1804) was a chasidic master named Jacob Kranz.

About the Author

Steven M. Rosman was ordained at Hebrew Union College and received his Ph.D. in Education from New York University with specializations in developmental theory and uses of story and imagery in education and religious settings. In December 1990 he was selected as Governor Mario Cuomo's featured storyteller at the Winter Holiday celebration at the state capital.

Rabbi Rosman is the author of six books: *Sidra Stories: A Torah Companion, Deena the Damselfly, When Your Child Asks You Why: Answers for Tough Questions* (with Kerry Olitzky and David Kasakove), *Eight Tales for Eight Nights*, which he co-wrote with Peninnah Schram, *Spiritual Parenting: A Guide for Parents and Teachers*, and *The Bird of Paradise and Other Sabbath Stories*.

Rabbi Rosman has spent two years studying the healing wisdom of the world's great religious traditions to earn the degree of spiritual counselor. He currently serves as rabbi of the Jewish Family Congregation in South Salem, New York, and is married with two children.

About the Artist

Josepha Silman is an artist, graphic designer, writer, and fashion illustrator. She was born in Israel and has studied at the Corcoran School of Art in Washington, DC, and at the School of Visual Arts in New York City. Currently she conducts a mural-art workshop.